Uprising
In
East Germany

and other stories
by JOCHEN ZIEM

Uprising In East Germany

and other stories

by JOCHEN ZIEM

Translated from the German by
Jorn K. Bramann and Jeanette Axelrod

ADLER PUBLISHING COMPANY, ROCHESTER, NY

UPRISING IN EAST GERMANY and Other Stories

BY JOCHEN ZIEM

Some of the stories in this collection originally published in *Zahltage*, © 1968 Suhrkamp Verlag and *Die Klassefrau*, © 1974, Hermann Luchterhand Verlag.

First American Edition

English translation copyright © 1985
by Adler Publishing Company

For information address
Adler Publishing Company
P.O. Box 9342
Rochester, New York 14604

Translated by Jorn K. Bramann and Jeanette Axelrod

Cover illustration after the lithograph "Fassade"
by Peter Umlauf

Cover Design by Sasha Trouslot / Foxglove Graphics.

ISBN 0-913623-07-5
NIGHTSUN #5 (1985)
ISSN 0278-6079

Library of Congress Catalog Card No. 84-71439

Printed in the United States of America

89   88   87   86   85   5   4   3   2   1

TABLE OF CONTENTS

STATEMENT

My attorney has informed me that I do not have to respond to the fantasies of an eleven year old girl. They're outrageous. I was never really too crazy about Margot. She acted too old for her age. From behind she looked like a fifteen year old slut from the sticks. Her mother took her too seriously, which wasn't surprising since her father had left them.

I am not saying anything against Mrs. Lehmbrock. I'm even grateful to her. Not many landladies will accept a musician with a grand piano these days. But Mrs. Lehmbrock always told her daughter too much about herself and her husband. I heard it with my own ears. A kid has no business being told about who her father slept with. It only encourages a sick imagination, and what she wrote about me can only be described that way. It's ridiculous.

I'm sticking to what I said in my deposition. At the most, I can only add a few more things.

Mrs. Lehmbrock will confirm that I was an agreeable tenant. When I moved in, I told her: You don't have to worry about me practising all the time. I'm not a concert pianist. I'm the quiet type. The most I'll do is figure out a few variations on a new hit. When you sit at the piano night after night you need some peace and quiet during the day. Also, I always pay my rent on time.

I was glad to get away from Frankfurt and find work in Baden. Those G.I. bars had been getting to me for awhile. I was happy to be able to move into a quiet and well kept place like Mrs. Lehmbrock's. I felt like a human being again. There has never been any trouble between us.

Once in a while Mrs. Lehmbrock invited me to lunch. The kid was usually not around, since she ate lunch at school. Mrs. Lehmbrock mostly talked about her marriage, which had failed, and I listened to her but in order not to give her any false hopes, I let her know that I had no trouble finding women for myself. It's really disgusting how certain women look at me over the shoulders of their dancing partners while I play the piano, with unmistakable meaning in their eyes. And sometimes, if I feel like encouraging them a little, I know certain tricks. George Shearing is a sure winner with older women. I do Errol Garner for the younger ones. That's why I'm still a bachelor at thirty-eight. It's difficult to meet decent women in my line of work.

Whatever the case may be, I told Mrs. Lehmbrock all of these things and we maintained our mutual respect.

My relationship with Margot was entirely normal and I will state that this was the way it was until her deplorable death. If the girl imagined things, that was her problem.

Of course I'll take care of the girl, I told Mrs. Lehmbrock when she came to me with tears in her eyes and a telegram in her hand. I understood completely when she explained that she had to go to Cologne right away in order to prevent another woman from claiming her inheritance. Margot and I took her to the railroad station. (I realized Margot was a pretty tough cookie when she didn't seem to be too moved by her father's death.) That was on Sunday.

We took a taxi back, sat down in the kitchen and had breakfast. Naturally, I wasn't too enthusiastic. The bar I was working in had just closed down for a week of remodeling and I had six days off. I'd thought of doing all kinds of things, but sometimes sacrifices are necessary, particularly if you're being treated nicely. I thought: The brat is old enough to stay home by herself at night, so at least I won't have to watch her then.

Margot got some salmon and liver pie from the refrigerator and toast from the sideboard. We ate, drank milk and Margot giggled constantly for no reason. Suddenly, she demanded: Ask me whether I already have a boyfriend!

I wondered: Why am I supposed to ask that question?

Come on, ask it! she begged.

So I asked her whether she already had a boyfriend.

She gave me that sly smirk of hers and asked: Why do you want to know?

But I don't want to know! I said.

You really don't want to know?

No, really! I said. Margot kept looking at me in a way that embarrassed me.

Then we went down to the garden. It was the first sunny day in April and I took off my shirt and settled down in a recliner. Suddenly Margot was standing next to me wearing nothing but a pair of flimsy beach shorts. Her mother really should have told her that it was time for her to wear a bra, or at least a shirt. But it wasn't my business to tell Mrs. Lehmbrock how to educate her daughter.

Margot said: On Sundays, my mother always brushes my hair! She had already undone her braids and she held out her brush in front of me, so I brushed her blond hair. Whenever I said that I'd done it enough, she just cooed and begged.

It didn't take much effort to overlook the swellings of her breasts, which were still covered with down. If that child wrote in her diary that I made tender advances, I must insist that I didn't do anything more than I would have done if I'd been absent-mindedly petting a cat.

Since I wanted to go into the city, I put her to bed rather early. I don't know why I didn't really feel like doing anything that night – even when I was already on the bus. When the bus reached the end of the line at the Augustaplatz, I just stayed on board and rode back. Margot was standing in the hallway, shivering. Tears were beaded on her eyelashes.

I took her in my arms and comforted her. She hadn't slept, she whimpered, but her eyes were swollen with sleep. She said that she was scared because something was moving around the house.

I put her back to bed, tucked her in and talked to her soothingly. I thought: She'll be asleep in a minute. But she suddenly sat up and said: I just can't fall asleep. Could I come up to your apartment and sleep on the couch in the front room?

I wanted things to finally quiet down so I carried her, with all her bedding, upstairs. I wondered why her body was so strangely cramped. It felt as if I were putting a wooden board down on the couch.

I went into the other room, finished reading my detective story and drank half a bottle of wine. It was still rather early when I went to bed. Margot was asleep; at least that's what I thought. I leafed through the newspaper before I turned off the light. Just as I was dozing off into my first dream, a strange vibrating sound came from the wall across the room and woke me up again. Since I couldn't figure out what it was, I lay still for a while and listened until it finally became clear that the sound was coming from the couch.

I thought to myself: Maybe she's thrown off her covers and is shivering in the cold. So I went in and turned on the light. Why shouldn't I admit it? What I saw confused me. At first I wanted to turn off the light immediately, but since she'd turned her face away and kept her eyes closed, I thought: Pretend you don't understand. I went over, put her hand aside, pulled her nightgown down to her knees and pulled the blanket up to her shoulders. Go to sleep now! I said. Nothing else. I didn't want to scare her.

The next morning I must have slept through the alarm. I didn't wake up till noon. Margot didn't come home from school until the afternoon. When I asked her where she'd been, she gave me a fresh answer. Every time I looked at her she blushed and was in a hurry to get away. I found that amusing, of course, but at the same time I felt sorry for her. To spare her the necessity of avoiding me, I went straight over to her.

She was sitting at her desk in front of a math book, licking her pen. I told her: You don't have to have a guilty conscience. We've all been your age once! Margot pretended that she wasn't listening and I didn't pay any more attention to her.

That night I wanted to go into the city again. I reminded her to act reasonably and she earnestly nodded in agreement. But then she suddenly yelled after me: Are you going to get laid?

Do you mind? I asked. I had to laugh, because she was moving her body like a woman in bed.

I ran into a woman at the casino – one of those tramps – who invited me to her place. True, I didn't get home until the next morning after Margot had already left for school, but it's still annoying to be compared to those studs who'd been with that broad yesterday or the day before.

The sun was shining again. The mountains began to turn green and the buds on the trees were bulging. I went up to the roof garden and lay out on a blanket, naked. Suddenly Margot was standing behind me and asked: What are you doing?

I covered myself with a towel, but Margot, without any invitation, slammed an air mattress down beside me and undressed. When I'm with mom at the North Sea, she said, we always go to the nudist beach.

I fell asleep, but not for long since Margot was drawing a tickling black line with her pen from my armpit to my waist. I grabbed her to give her a slap on the ass, but she whimpered: Please don't hit me! I won't do it again!

I was stupid enough to oblige. For hardly had I let go of her hands when she drew a second line from my breast to my belly button. This time she was faster and got away before I could grab her. I couldn't chase her because the wall around the roof was too low to give me any cover from the neighbors' view.

Margot made fun of me, but when she saw from the expression on my face that I was not amused anymore, she begged for peace.

For ten minutes she pretended to be a good girl and did her homework. Distracted, I wasn't quick enough to stop her from drawing a third line – this time from my knee to my upper thigh. But I did manage to grab her arm, not caring if she screamed. First I slapped her ass; then, because she tried to tickle me, I began to tickle her. That wasn't easy, since she fought back and tried to bite and scratch me. She pulled my hair and clawed herself into my waist and shoulder. She pressed her knee under my chin and into my stomach. We rolled on top of each other a few times, quite innocently to be sure. The concrete floor beyond the blanket and the mattress scraped our skin. We landed on my blanket again, exhausted, I on my back and Margot sitting on my out-stretched leg. We panted and laughed, and Margot, when she caught her breath again, threw up her arms and yelled: Victory!

I admitted defeat so she looked for her pen and started drawing on me again. I thought: Let her! I have to clean up anyway.

First she carefully drew circles around my nipples, and then enclosed them in spirals. Then she turned to my navel, drew a circle around it, a nose and eyes above it and made it look like a singing mouth. She finally expanded the face into a sun, drawing rays all over my belly. She was totally absorbed in her artistry – I cannot emphasize enough that I did not suspect anything at all.

Only when she slid down to my shin to draw on my thigh did I tell her: Quit it! For when she moved down my leg she left a moist trail, as if a snail had crawled on it. That shocked me, of course, and I turned over to lie on my stomach. That's why I can't be sure whether she noticed that something had stirred me up. In her diary, she just fantasized about it, like everything else.

I took a shower. Then we ate in the kitchen. Margot asked me several times whether I had enjoyed the afternoon the way she had, and whether I was still mad at her. And then she wanted to know if I had found a woman last night and what had I done with her. Margot kept busy serving peppermint tea and her voice sounded as if her tonsils were swollen.

Of course I didn't tell her anything. I just said that I had met an acquaintance. I didn't reveal the slightest detail of that night—that would have been against my principles. Besides, children shouldn't be told things like that. That stuff Margot scribbled in her diary is just vicious. I couldn't have even possibly told her those things since my acquaintance isn't the type to do what was described.

The next afternoon, Margot came home with a friend, a scrawny girl with skinny legs and slanted eyes. I didn't like her at all and I was afraid that she would get Margot to do something stupid. It became ominously quiet in the house. When I didn't hear those brats at all, I went downstairs to Margot's room. I didn't exactly sneak up to the room but I must have been wearing my rubber soled shoes. In any event, they both blushed when I came into the room. They were sitting on Margot's bed, with their backs to the wall and their legs hidden under the quilt.

Are you cold? I asked.

Margot replied: Oh, just a little.

The other girl grinned impertinently and said: Margot's been telling me some interesting things.

Shut up! Margot said, jabbing her elbow into the girl's ribs.

Later, when Margot came back after taking her friend to the bus stop, I confronted her. I hope you're not spreading around any nonsense, I said. Margot went to the kitchen, shoved half a cucumber

into her mouth and wouldn't look at me. She said:
I'm allowed to tell the truth, aren't I?

Of course you are! I said. You're even supposed to.

Margot walked to the front of the stove and stirred
the milk pot, with her back turned to me for an
annoyingly long time. Then she said in that sly tone
of voice: Can I also tell my mother?

I replied: Do what you like. But if you tell any lies,
I'll get rough with you! I never said: I'll kill you!
How could I say that to a child? Never! Not even as
a joke.

I was angry and paced up and down in my room. I
opened a bottle of red wine and drank a few glasses,
but it didn't agree with my stomach. It wasn't very
good wine; cheap Algerian stuff. Usually I can hold
a lot more, but that night I wasn't in good shape so I
just went to bed early. Even Carter Brown bored
me, and he usually gives me a lift.

I must have fallen asleep. Suddenly Margot was
standing behind my bed, staring at me silently. I
said: What do you want?

You don't have to be afraid that I'll tell my mother
about it, she said.

That was too much for me. Listen! I said. First of
all, I am not afraid. And second, you can say what
you want. What on earth do you want to tell her,
anyway, that's so mysterious?

She just chewed on her lip, pouted and stared
intensely at a particular spot on my body. I think I

even blushed. I lost control of myself and yelled: Are you imagining that you and I did anything together? Since she didn't say anything and just shrugged her shoulders, I slapped her in the face.

She held her face in her hands and ran downstairs. Of course I felt sorry for her right away. For a while I thought about how I could make up for the slap in the face and whether I should buy her some chocolates, a book or a doll. And then I thought: Why not go down and tell her that I didn't mean it? I put on my bathrobe.

I could hear her sobbing from out in the hall. I knocked, groped my way to her bed and told her not to make such a scene. I sat down beside her and dried her tears, talked to her calmly and held her hand. But she didn't stop crying and finally told me that her stomach hurt. I put my hand on her belly and let it circle smoothly – the way my mother used to do when I was hurting with a stomach ache. Margot did, in fact, quiet down right away.

My head was still fuzzy from the cheap wine . . . You have to get up or you'll fall asleep . . . , I thought to myself. It's possible that it was all a dream. It was almost two o'clock when I woke up and was shocked because I couldn't remember how the child had gotten next to me. I tiptoed upstairs, hoping that she'd fallen asleep before I did. I couldn't have known that her imagination was wild enough to fantasize things that embarrass me from beginning to end. I definitely want to mention that I was firmly wrapped in my bathrobe and I doubt very much if I had been lying under her covers.

The telegraph messenger woke me up. I was relieved to learn that Mrs. Lehmbrock was returning that night. I was tired of playing nanny and besides, I was scheduled to work again on Sunday. Since it was a warm, almost cloudless day, I sunbathed again on the roof garden – but this time in trunks. When Margot came home in the afternoon I even put on a shirt.

Margot hung around me constantly. First she played with a ball and bounced it next to me until I finally knocked it over the wall, down into the garden. Then she came at me with a clothesline, rolled it like a lasso and tried to capture my toes. After the line landed in the garden as well, she tried to play acrobat, balancing on top of the narrow wall. I warned her several times, asking her to come down. She said: I do this all the time. And she added: If you're afraid I'll fall, why don't you come over and lift me down?

There must have been a loose brick that upset her balance. I still see her in front of me, flailing her arms. I jump up and race towards her. She falls. I grab for her leg but only get hold of her shoe. Her foot slides out before I can catch it with my other hand.

If I hadn't tried to catch her, she probably would have fallen on her side or maybe on her legs. It might have ended up with nothing worse that a few broken bones. But when I tried to hold her by her foot, her whole body turned over and she hit the stone floor of the terrace head on.

That is the only thing I can reproach myself for, but it can't be held against me legally.

I immediately rushed down to her and although I could see right away that she was dead, I called the ambulance and rode with the body to the clinic. I stayed with her until Mrs. Lehmbrock arrived.

I had a whole night to make that diary disappear, but since I had a clear conscience, I didn't even look for it. I admit that if I had known what she'd written in it, the book wouldn't exist anymore.

But however that may be, this is all I have to say.

I have no comment concerning the results of the autopsy, although it doesn't surprise me. In any event, I had nothing to do with it.

SOMETHING'S MISSING

Sure, he could change his job. He's seen television shows on those exploration teams that drilled for oil in the desert. That interested him.

He also thought about going to South Africa, or the Congo. They need mechanics there. He could even bring his family along. He says that this would be an advantage. But it isn't just the job.

There is, of course, no doubt that right now he's stuck in one of the dumbest jobs around: heating systems installation. It's really ridiculous. So he's team leader, and the men respect him. So he's making good money. One of these days he'll quit anyway. The trouble is that quitting won't solve anything. He's afraid that he'll just end up spending Friday nights down at the bar again, playing cards with his buddies—or bowling, while the wives sit around, chatting about God and the world, drinking peppermint schnapps and believing that they're having one hell of a good time.

He hadn't thought that it would be this way—back then when he came home. And the worst part of it is . . . he can't talk about it. When he tries, they all seem to listen, and they say things like: Fantastic! and Weird!—but in the end they shrug and look embarrassed because they don't really know what he means. The most they'd say is: What are you complaining about? You've never had it so good! And, he says, they're not really wrong.

His kid is two years old now. The little bugger races

through the apartment like a hurricane and talks non-stop. Even in French. He only speaks French to the kid. One of his buddies' kids has a brain disease. The child is retarded and vicious besides. He reminds Waltraud about this child whenever she gets upset over their own kid's demolition of another one of her crystal pieces.

He's been lucky with Waltraud too, he reflects. Back when they couldn't find an apartment she immediately agreed to become manager and superintendant of an apartment house. Now, he assures her that he is perfectly able to rent an apartment without those obligations, but she doesn't care. She doesn't mind taking care of the whole building, and she doesn't neglect her family because of her job either. When he comes home from work, she never says things like: I still have to do the stairway. He saves a lot of money because of her. Waltraud knows how to keep the money together too, without scrimping on food. And she's never made a scene when he'd come home plastered. That's why he's so sorry that he gave her a black eye yesterday.

Waltraud blames it on television. Maybe she's right, he says. When they showed that movie on Saigon last night, he could tell her a story about every streetcorner. And after the part about the attack on Plei Ku, he just sat up in the living room until three in the morning, going through five bottles of beer. Waltraud didn't sleep well and kept coming in every two hours, asking him what was wrong, was he thinking about those oriental women, or if not, what was it he was thinking about.

He says that she doesn't understand a thing. Yesterday, he gave it another try. On Sundays he likes to drive out to the hills east of here. He knows a place between Haag and Ohligs where even on Sundays there are few tourists; a range of hills with some woods on top, wheat and potato fields on the slopes and a brush-lined creek running through the hollow. The dust from the dirt roads dries the mucous in his nostrils just as fast as the winds on the high plain of Da Nang had, where they had to pull the stuff out of their noses every half-hour. But it isn't just the dust that makes him so tense, which causes this change in him. Waltraud would walk beside him like an alarmed nurse. She'd say: You're acting funny! She notices his tension, especially when they encounter other people — a farmer, a woman, or anyone else taking a Sunday walk. He'd always been very scared. Just like Kraag and Schlettschick . . . after all, no day ever passed without at least one of the Legionnaires getting killed this way. You couldn't trust anyone . . . not the old man dragging his feet between crutches, not the group of women carrying bundles on their heads or babies on their backs and, least of all the nine to fifteen year old boys, strolling by with big grins on their faces.

At first, he, Kraag and Schlettschick had always put their submachine guns into position, releasing the safeties. But after a while they learned to recognize from the way someone walked whether or not the bundle on their head was a cover for a gun or whether a girl's rice bowl contained a grenade. Sometimes they started shooting out of sheer nervousness — because they couldn't stand the suspense when someone came along at an especially

slow pace. He himself mostly shot above the heads of
the passersby, just to see what would happen. It was
risky, of course, but there was also something
sporting about it. Kraag and Schlettschick hadn't
indulged in that luxury. Schlettschick was rather
lazy. His motto was: Better ten times in vain than
once too late! — but what a way he had of unscrewing
his canteen afterwards!

Waltraud doesn't understand this. Perhaps, he says,
she doesn't have enough imagination to understand
that men need a drink after a close call, even if it
really hadn't been all that bad. He suspects a lack
of fantasy in her — a farmer in his Sunday suit,
nicely dressed country girls, two boys on bicycles
with their tents strapped to the carriers — for her,
these people are just what they seem to be. She
absolutely refuses to see anything else in them. But
to see the way he saw would be the only way in
which she could get an idea of how he had lived back
then. He says that she even gets into a bad mood
when she has to pack sandwiches on Sundays, and
climb into the Volkswagen bus — even though he
always spreads a blanket over the seat. There's no
way she could soil her dress on the oil spots that the
mechanics left. As long as he's allowed to take the
company bus home every night and use it for
personal trips on the weekends, he wouldn't dream
of buying his own car. He can always do that later.
He used to have to make do with all kinds of
unbelievable wrecks and was glad if they ran at all,
so he can't take Waltraud's dislike for the company
bus, with it's blue and white lettering, all that
seriously. Waltraud, of course, would prefer to get
all dressed-up and sit in one of those fancy cafes
along the Rhine, feeding the kid cake. Sometimes

he thought about going to the hills without
Waltraud, but he couldn't bring himself to leave his
family alone on a Sunday.

So she just has to bear with him as he crouches in a
ditch, watching the hillside attentively; not to be
interrupted in his thoughts.

He told her again yesterday: Imagine them coming
down from up there, out of those woods. First you
see three, then five, then fifteen. And by the time
you've stopped counting them to get the guns and
ammunition boxes ready, you realize that at least
half of them are already half-way down the hill,
wearing camouflage that blends into the landscape
like leaves of grass in a meadow. You have to pay
close attention to even notice that something's
coming. Very close attention. Then you hear the
splashing to the right and left. You already know
their technique of running, throwing themselves
down and shooting. And you know that they're
noisy on purpose; they're scared shitless and they're
lousy shots. But that's only a comforting thought
until the first one starts howling and splashing
around or until one of them starts going through
silent contortions — which, of course, doesn't happen
too often. Your eye tracks through the landscape
above the visor and you feel the recoil of the gun
against your shoulder. Sweat drips down off
Schlettschick's face, running across the grimaces he
always makes in sticky situations, while Kraag
handles his grenade launcher with the calm of a
land surveyor. This kind of thing can go on for
hours, he says. For hours! Do you know what I
mean?

When Waltraud answered: Be glad you're done with
all that! all he could do was stare at her and shake
his head. And once she replied: Why don't you join
the army, then?

Waltraud is pretty dense about this also, he says.
What would he do in the army? Sit around the
barracks, clean uniforms, stand at attention or yell
at a bunch of recruits who weren't dirty enough for
just coming in from field exercises? Or shoot blanks
during war games — become a member of a Shriner's
club gone haywire?

If Schlettschick could have heard that!   Even
Kraag, — who'd wanted to become an officer, but had
been cashiered by the Danish Army for some silly
reason — even Kraag declined to join the regular
French Army; although the opportunity was offered
to him, together with French citizenship. Today,
Kraag's in the Congo. But he'd bet that Kraag
would come right back if there were a civil war in
France. He himself would probably be in France for
the same reason: to bump off some French officers.
The officers ruined the Legion, he says. If the Legion
had been allowed to recruit from the ranks, he
swears things would look different in Vietnam
today.

He's thought about writing to the American
Embassy to offer his services. The Americans are
doing some good things down there; they certainly
don't fuck around. But Waltraud can't understand
this either. After every television report he wants to
explain things to her, to make her understand what
she sees through her uncomprehending eyes. She
just asks: What makes all this your business? He

believes, however, that all this is very much his business; for example, the American rescue operations—how they use helicopters to get their downed pilots out of the jungle or how they fish them out of the ocean. He remembers the episode with Kraag—Schlettschick was already dead by this time.

Under the leadership of a French lieutenant, they had set out with twelve men to explore a few hills. They only took light luggage—their rifles. First they marched for two hours along the rice paddies and through some miserable deserted villages. Finally they entered the woods and when the ferns in the underbrush became too thick, they walked single file along a narrow path. These paths always made him nervous and he usually avoided them. One reason he feared them was because you were set up like a pin in a bowling alley. The other reason was the mines. He kept to the side, chopping through the thickets with his bayonet. Suddenly someone screamed and a stretch of the path exploded. Two of them lay motionless in the grass; one had his spine torn by shrapnel, the other missing a leg and his forehead. That one must have looked down when the mine exploded. Only Kraag was still standing—in the pose of a runner. He seemed to be in the middle of a jump, yet he stood motionless, as if his foot had been nailed to the ground.

Instantly he realized what had happened to Kraag and the two others. Seasoned Indochina Legionnaires had warned him. They had advised him to always carry a little saw and never wear light shoes with rubber soles. He'd brushed off the advice as veterans' yarns, cheap propaganda. But Kraag's posture, his face, his cautiously balancing arm confirmed the treacherous nature of this kind of mine, made of handgrenades.

Fire started coming in from a distance. The lieutenant called in the men and those who followed his call disappeared with him into the brush. The lieutenant must have seen and understood what kept Kraag rooted to the spot. A slimy bastard, the lieutenant, he says. The type who only thinks of his missions, not his men.

He crawled over to Kraag who was pointing to his foot in horror and trying to motion him away. He told Kraag to squat down and keep quiet. A bloody bamboo spike stuck out of Kraag's right shoe and blood was running out from under the sole. The hook of the spike must have gotten stuck between Kraag's toe bones.

He didn't have a little saw with him, nor did Kraag. He couldn't find one on the dead soldiers either. It was impossible to carve through the spike with a bayonet because there wasn't enough room between the shoe and the ground, so he scraped the dirt off the top of the mine—dirt which had hardened in the dry season. Kraag wanted to do it himself, but he wouldn't let him. Kraag's fingers were trembling too much. He told Kraag to calm down and make sure he didn't move his foot unless it was absolutely necessary, and then only downward, even if it hurt like hell. Lifting the foot would detonate the mine and blow the whole thing in his face. The mine was nothing more than a wooden box, an ordinary box—not even the slightest resemblance to a mine.

It would have looked like a harmless crate if it hadn't been for Kraag's blood, which kept dripping from the spike.

And now . . . what? The shooting had stopped. Should he run to the last village to look for a saw — a fret saw, or something like it? But who knew what was left in a ransacked place like that. Besides, it would be a two hour trek plus another hour to comb through the huts. No, under the circumstances he had to use the bayonet. Only, bamboo has a damned smooth surface, almost impenetrable. You can't simply slash through it, but have to proceed with absolute caution; with incredible caution so that there won't be any jolt.

He wants to make it short — He sat beside the mine for two hours, cutting and scraping; it was like carving an ivory miniature with a meat cleaver. He was dripping wet, and his tongue felt like a grindstone. Kraag had put himself into a comfortable position, if comfortable is the right word, sitting on his ass with his left leg stretched out, his right one edged above the mine and his hand a support under his heel. He kept his face turned away. He himself didn't really want to see the mess either. He could very well imagine how it must feel to have a fishhook yanking at his nerves with every little bit of pressure from the bayonet, not to mention the powder keg beneath the foot. As he had said: two hours. Then he cut the shoe open and drove the severed spike upward through Kraag's toe. After he bandaged the wound, he made a splint for Kraag's leg out of pieces of wood.

It took them six hours to get back to camp. Only after he reported in did he notice that he hadn't spoken in all that time, that it hadn't been necessary. And he was amazed when he realized how much talk was really just shooting the breeze, just bullshit. The rest of the group never came back, which was to his advantage since he probably would have been courtmartialed for disobeying orders.

Kraag wasn't in the hospital for too long and when he got out he presented to him, without a word, a big bottle of Courvoisier VSOP. On a suitable evening they'd emptied it together and they hadn't talked much then either. And the drunker he got, the more he remembered the sounds of that afternoon — the scraping of the bayonet, Kraag's irregular breathing, and the cracking of his joints; once in a while a falling branch in the woods and time and again the scraping and the breathing.

Why is he talking about all this? He doesn't mean to brag. He isn't a hero. That's not how he's made, he says, and he certainly isn't longing for war. He could have, after all, gone to Algeria to serve another five year stint once things were wrapped up in Indochina. He didn't do it. By then he knew how things were going. But he thought things would be different at home: more happening, more . . . he doesn't know how to put it. He'd been eighteen, just finished with his apprenticeship, when he joined the Legion. He wanted adventure. And later, he thought: Those nights when you sit drinking Cognac and don't have to say anything because you've done something — those nights should be repeatable anywhere, any time.

Okay, he says, laying pipes in a big building, installing radiators that really get warm when someone opens the valve—that's not meaningless. He knows that. He can tell that to himself every morning at breakfast. And he's better paid for connecting pipes than he was for disconnecting Kraag from the mine. The Roman heating systems are still tourist attractions, and for good reason. Still . . .

And love. Okay, he has a nice kid, and life with Waltraud isn't boring by any means. But despite all this he still can't quite suppress his thoughts about the women over in Indochina. Not because they did anything special. They were no different from the women here. You get used to them after a while and the lure of the exotic fades away. Then they're just broads like anywhere else. But Schlettschick bought it, all because he fell asleep afterwards. They had all warned him, but Schlettschick would have found the whole act meaningless if he couldn't take a little snooze when he was finished. He was in Saigon with Schlettschick several times. They'd always been lucky, but you never really knew how things stood with those women—that was part of the fun. It was clear that they had to stay together and it was also clear that they never should have entered that maze of huts. But those two broads were the kind that were usually reserved for officers.

He'd had a funny feeling right away, and he put his submachine gun beside himself on the mat with exaggerated care. The woman just laughed. Not about him, but at him. She kind of smiled—and that's enough with those women. Schlettschick was lying in the other room. For a while he could hear him through the thin wall. He didn't listen all the time, of course, for his woman was far too good.

She finally got up and announced that she had to go pee. She'd be back in a minute, and then she'd continue. He immediately readied his gun. Then he called across the wall. There was no answer. He called again. Schlettschick! Wake up! Again, no answer. He went over — a few minutes too late. The blood from his slit throat had already slowed to a trickle.

That, of course, was too much for him.

He couldn't find anyone around the hut, but there was a group of people at the end of the alley, chattering in their sly, insidious way. The sight of them made him sick. He emptied his entire magazine into the crowd. He had never been like that before, he says.

He's sorry that he hit Waltraud, and in the eye, of all places. There's something demeaning, low-life, about a woman running around with a black eye. When he'd decided to write that letter to the American Embassy, just to be part of the whole thing once more, he certainly didn't have those oriental women in mind. In the end he hadn't written the letter anyway. Sure, the Americans are doing some impressive things over there. But it's also so mechanical. They aren't soldiers anymore, they're killing machine engineers. They don't rely that much on personal engagement — the kind of engagement needed when that boiler fell over.

It was some boiler that they had to move into the basement. They even had to take down a couple of walls! And suddenly the damn boiler started to fall. Klaus! he yelled. Klaus is fifteen, the company apprentice. He was standing there, daydreaming, and gave a start at the call, but then stumbled and fell. He lay there, the slowly tilting boiler right above him. The four men who had moved it downstairs weren't able to hold it any longer.

He saw how the thing was falling, he says, and the kid was lying right in its path. The men were frozen, horrified expressions on their faces. He instantly grabbed for an iron bar that was lying nearby and wedged it between the kid and the falling mass of steel. The bar could have splintered, in which case he would have had it too, but luckily he'd wedged it in at a good angle. The bar bent on impact and slowly kept on bending. The kid managed to get up in time and dash out of danger — he was right behind him just as the bar gave out.

After quitting time he took the kid out for a schnapps, and then delivered him to his parents. Don't get him wrong — he didn't take the kid home in order to receive his parents' thanks. A handshake was enough for him, and the few words his men had come up with.

Waltraud had to sit down. She called it: Irresponsible! Foolhardy! She just doesn't understand things like that.

The problem is, he says, that he can't spend all his time waiting for some boiler to fall over.

THE CLASSY WOMAN

He's got a lot to learn now. He's already read *Wage, Price, and Profit* by Marx, and Engels' *Origin of the Family,* and more besides. Every time he thinks that it's finally clicked, that he's got it down, Hertha tells him not to get any notions. Hertha simply knows more, and this difference in their education spooks him. When they plow through a book together, Hertha is always far ahead of him. She understands quicker. And most of all, she remembers what she's read, while his difficulties begin with the alphabet. When he looks up a foreign word in the dictionary, he always has to rattle down the ABC's the way he had been drilled to do in grade school. And when Hertha comforts him, telling him that memory is just a matter of exercise, he just gets a sinking feeling in the pit of his stomach because she's had so many more years of exercise than he has.

He's got to catch up with her. He's just bought himself five volumes of *The History of the German Labor Movement* and he knows that this is really heavy, but he doesn't want Hertha to be ashamed of him. Everywhere they go she tells people that he's twenty-two. He's really twenty-six. But she thinks that by making him younger, his lack of education won't be such a liability.

Sometimes he tells himself: Claus, throw in the towel! Hit the road! Get yourself a chick who'll keep her mouth shut, wash your socks, and spread her legs without making a big deal out of it. And he might have quit the whole business already if

Hertha wasn't such a good lay. If he's learned anything, it's that the old saw: Stupidity is good for fucking—it just isn't true, and he thinks that Hertha has some appreciation for his sexual performance as well. It isn't true that he's insensitive, as Hertha sometimes says. Before he puts his dick into her he always massages her for half an hour, leaving no muscle in her untouched. She can say what she wants— she comes. You can hear her coming with everything she's got. He may get thrown out of his apartment one of these days because she's so loud. When they go at it at two in the morning, it's always a pretty noisy affair and sometimes outraged neighbors pound on his door. But that only gets him more excited. Actually, he could fuck Hertha any time of the day, morning, noon or night—if he only had the time.

Unfortunately she doesn't always want to fuck. She often has a headache, a backache, a bellyache or she just has her "problems." When she has her "problems" she sits in front of the T.V. from morning till midnight, or she lies in bed with her face against the wall, screaming at him when he as much as touches her. When she's like this, he retreats into the kitchen. But he thinks: a guy shouldn't live with a woman like that just to end up doing it by himself! He does, of course, whack off when Hertha is away on a trip. Why go to the trouble of hauling in some piece of ass? Besides, he's developed a certain feeling of loyalty towards Hertha. But when he lies beside her thinking: she really could do it now, and she talks about her "problems" instead, he just can't sympathize. If she would only explain to him what the hell her "problems" are! On days like this he goes to the nearest bar and knocks back one beer after another.

He knows that at first he'd meant nothing more to Hertha than a left-wing kick. In the penitentiary, a poet had shown up one day and read a lot of weird stuff: that everything in this society was just a pile of shit—and things like that. He had known that since he was ten years old, when they sent him to a home for juvenile delinquents. Someone had broken his father's neck in a bar brawl, and his mother took to sending him through the stores to steal groceries. Nobody knew what on earth the poet wanted from them: a fortyish hippie with long hair, headband and the face of an old maid.

When they let him out of the joint, he looked up the poet. He was amazed at how eager the poet was to see him again, but on the table, next to the bottle of Cognac, there was a tape recorder. Claus smelled something fishy, so all he said was that he just needed a room, or a small apartment. But in order to get one, he had to answer ads, which meant he also needed a neatly typed letter to impress the landlords. Would that be asking too much from a poet?

The poet sat at his desk for forty-five minutes, thinking, writing and emptying a bottle of red wine. Then he called Hertha, who came in from another room. In a foul mood, she typed out ten copies and bitched about not being the poet's secretary.

There was a lot of room in the poet's apartment. He would have preferred to crash there instead of going home to his mother, but the atmosphere was so tense, and some kind of blow-up seemed so close, that he quickly took the letters and got out of there. He really should have been grateful! The first four letters he sent to the morning paper got him a small apartment in the North of Berlin; a room with kitchen and a coke burning stove. Nothing fancy, but still . . .

A second appointment with the poet slipped his mind. A few weeks after that, Claus met him in a bar. The poet was swaying in front of a pinball machine, staring at the "tilt" sign, unaware that he was already playing with Hertha's ball. Hertha moved her man away from the machine and put him on a chair. Then she turned and asked Claus if he wanted to finish the game with her. He noticed that she was spreading a little in the butt and that her face was also on the broad side, but that she had unusually alert eyes. She asked how he was and what he was doing. What am I supposed to be doing? he said, I'm holding down a job! What else can I do? She wanted him to be more specific. What was he doing this Saturday night? Don't know yet, he replied. Maybe some joy-riding. But that was just bragging. He doesn't know how to drive. He's had his worst experiences with cars.

When he was still living at the Home, just after finishing school, he'd been allowed to work in a gas station. He could keep one mark a day for himself, but every week he made up to twenty-five marks in tips on the side. He could afford cigarettes, boys who'd give him a blow-job, and something which no other kid in the Home could afford: a drink once in a while. Then one day he decided to take a ride in a Volkswagen which had been left parked after going through the station's car-wash. But he put it into second instead of reverse and smashed it into a wall. That experience is still with him. A real trauma!

Hertha said that before he stole her car for a joyride, she'd rather give him the keys herself for an hour or so. He gave the keys back to her, saying he was too loaded to drive. Right now, he said, swimming sounds better than driving!

It was a warm night. They drove out to Lake Glienicke and went skinny-dipping. Couples were lying all over the place, filling the air with sounds of passion. Cautiously, he reached for her neck. She came around faster than he expected. They kissed and necked like maniacs; her saliva tasted like bitter almonds.

He doesn't want to lie—he was scared shitless. Until then the only kind of chick he'd had would either just lie there or put up some resistance before getting turned on, but he'd never had a woman over thirty who let him know so matter-of-factly that she wanted it right then and there! He beat a hasty retreat, looking for excuses—that it was getting late and cold. He was impressed when she didn't seem to hold it against him.

She dropped him off at his place. He told her that all he had was an air mattress in his apartment. The next day she went with him to the Kreuzberg flea market, buying and hauling back mattresses, a couple of chairs, pots, dishes and other household goods. And when his place was freshly painted and arranged, she brought him flowers and a vase. He told her how great he thought she was, and that there was really only one more thing that he could wish for—that he could make love to her. Hertha undressed immediately and joined him on his mattress, making it a perfect day.

He doesn't want to deceive himself, though — he
knows he hadn't won Hertha over from the poet. He
also knows that he's not bad looking and Hertha also
tells him that she likes his body, but he's not stupid,
even though he lacks an education.   Hertha's
relationship with that pitiful poet had already been
on the rocks.   Hertha told him that the guy got
drunk every night, and did nothing but babble away
for hours about the liberation of the working class,
although he never really did anything about it.
Claus figured that Hertha had just waited for the
best chance to jump ship, and that chance happened
to be him.

Don't get any ideas now, he told himself. Keep your
feet on the ground.   That woman will come back
three or four times at the most.   And when Hertha
announced after three weeks that she was going to
Cannes to her ex-husband's summer home for a six
week vacation, he thought: Let go, let go! When she
asked him to come along, he thought she was only
being polite.

When he was a kid, the welfare agency once sent
him to a summer camp on the North Sea, and once
he had been on a camping trip with a buddy at the
Lido di Jesolo in Italy.   It was there that he'd
decided that he would never put his buns into that
kind of meat market or swim in that kind of sewer
again; he'd rather stay at the lakes of Berlin. This
was the extent of his previous travel experiences.

They wound their way through the Provence and the
Maritime Alps, a hot and fascinating landscape.
Hertha was a fabulous driver! Time and again he
asked himself what he should think of himself.

Should he pat himself on the back? Was he something really special? Or was he just a bought stud, a temporary dick for hire?

No, not even that! he thought when he first saw the house in Cannes. This house was built for someone else's dick than mine! In the past he'd always thought that whitewashed walls were something for the poor. The ceiling beams were black and the furniture, too, was entirely black and white. It was all canvas, leather, plastic or old, polished wood. And then, the kitchen! And the garden with its view of the Mediterranean!

Hertha did some shopping. Spices, most of all, because a human being just can't eat food without spices. Spices which Claus had never even heard of: Basil, Rosemary, Sage, Oregano, Thyme, Saffron, Cumin, Chervil, Mugwort, Ginger, Bay Leaves. At home, he hadn't known anything except salt and dusty pepper. And when salad did come with a meal, the leaves were just dunked in vinegar and sweetened with sugar. But that Hertha! She stirred mustard into oil, added lemon juice, salt, a dash of sugar, garlic, and a whole bunch of fresh herbs. She also washed the lettuce and sacrificed a fresh towel to get the leaves dry again so that they'd stay nice and crisp. Finally, a few drops of hot sauce—That's Orson Welles' secret recipe, she said.

She told him: Don't go crazy over this house, don't go around praising everything. After all, this bunker is owned by a real slime who made his bread by being a coward, a conformist, an advertising executive—if that isn't the ultimate shit! Whatever that kind puts together shouldn't be admired. It should be used, exploited!

He didn't understand what she meant by all that.

During the first few days he went from window to window and from chair to chair, trying out everything. From every corner of the terrace to the garden there were always new views to be appreciated. He almost went crazy. Finally, Hertha yelled at him. Damn it, stop behaving like a small time gardener touring Versailles for the first time. The guy who owns all this is a gaping asshole, and he made his money by kissing other people's asses!

At this point he finally yelled back at her. She had, after all, been married to that asshole, and had helped him build and furnish this luxury barn, and had hung out here every summer for years. She must have experienced at least a little bit of happiness around here — and in the company of that asshole, and with her own royal ass browned in the gorgeous sun of the Cote d' Azur!

No, she had never been happy, Hertha yelled back. That asshole had exploited her as long as her body had turned him on. Then he'd found someone else, but the sneak kept it a secret. He'd instigated her to have an affair, because, he told her, she should have an affair to prove her own independence, and to keep a young marriage young and suspenseful. She had had an affair, and then that asshole said that he couldn't stand it, that it was destroying him, that he'd been wrong. He'd cried, filed for divorce, and she still hadn't known that he'd had another woman all that time. He's paying her eight hundred marks a month, although by now he's earning ten times as much.

Hertha talked herself into a frenzy, drinking red wine until she got loaded. Then she smashed the last half bottle against the white wall. The wall looked pretty bad. He got out a sponge and washed it down and told her that she wouldn't get a penny from him if she pulled that kind of shit in his house.

At first Hertha laughed at him, saying that all he'd ever have was a miserable little shack on the outskirts of Berlin. Then, for the first time, she used the word "primitive" to describe him. He's sure he would have beaten the living crap out of her if she hadn't started to cry at the same time. He can't hit a crying woman. He just put her to bed.

During the next two days they didn't do anything but eat, fuck and swim. They only talked when it was absolutely necessary. When they were thoroughly tired out, she began to work on his head. She asked the weirdest questions — whether he was unionized, did he have class consciousness, what were his ideas on organizing the masses, what did he and his buddies think about conspicuous consumption — a whole load of really obnoxious questions. He thought to himself: This mother really has gone off the deep end; she isn't playing with a full deck. She lives in this mansion and keeps pestering me about exploitation and the class struggle! He asked her what was bothering her about exploitation and who put all this stuff into her head. Martin, she answered, her ex-husband. Martin once sang a different tune — before he was bought off by the advertising industry. He replied that she should be glad that Martin had sold out, if it could buy her a life like this. No, she snapped back, she wasn't going to be bought off. He told her not to open her mouth so wide. As far as he could tell, she was pretty damn lazy and quite nicely bought off.

He hoped that with this last remark, the whole chapter would be closed. But Hertha continued to probe: on the beach in Nice, in the Picasso Museum in Antibes, in the Leger Museum, in the pottery town of Vallauris, or during walks through Grasse. Frankly, he'd been insulted when Hertha tried to make him feel insecure in the middle of all those gorgeous olive, fig and cypress trees and fantastic ancient ruins. It reminded him of his grandmother's crazy compulsion: that woman had to stop whenever she saw a cat and say: Nice kitty, kitty, kitty. The cats never were impressed; they simply ran off. But his grandmother never learned and kept on doing it.

Still, at one point something clicked in his head. He had to admit that his father had been a real proletarian.   And even though the Home and penitentiary had taught him quite a bit, for him, as Hertha says, there had been no equal opportunity to move up in the world. That day he felt like a real ass – sitting in front of the Mediterranean, and at his back the gorgeous villa.

He told Hertha that the two weeks were up and his vacation was almost over. He didn't want to lose his job, so he planned to hitchhike back. She went into her yelling act again: Has she worked on his head all this time only to watch him act like a petty bourgeois shit-brain now? Why the hell should he care about his crappy company?   Aren't there enough other outfits around? Does he have to feel responsible for something he doesn't own?

He replied that he couldn't change the vacation rules from down there. Besides, one of his buddies would have to forgo his vacation if he stayed away, and last, if not least, he was broke. He doesn't want to be kept by a woman who's kept by her ex-husband.

Catching four rides, he made Lyon in a day. That night, he sat in the same cafe where Hertha had bought him his first Pernod. He bought himself a German newspaper. A kindly old man came over to his table and asked: What's happening in Germany these days? No idea, he replied, I haven't been there for two weeks. The old man said: I haven't been back there for thirty years. How does a young German like France these days? It's wonderful, Claus said, I'd almost like to stay. Nothing easier than that, the old man replied, all he had to do was look behind him.

An elderly lady was seated at the next table—all powdered and painted and draped from top to bottom in fancy clothes. If he'd approach that lady ... The old man intimated that in this way many had stayed in France. No way! he answered. That old bag is too made-up and the maggots are probably doing a number on her already. A state of advanced putrefaction! If anything, I'd rather have that young chick sitting next to her.

He had said all of this in his normal voice, since he assumed that nobody around there would understand him. But the young woman, a gorgeous girl with red hair and blue eyes, looked at him and smiled. She had understood him perfectly well: her grandparents lived in Dresden. He moved over to

her table.   An hour later they were in bed in her
room and he stayed with her for three days.   He
went to the country with Odile to visit her relatives
where they were having a birthday party.   Everyone
sat around a huge wooden table in the middle of a
lovely garden, gorging themselves with food and
drink.   He kept piling in the food, got loaded and
then they went off and fucked their brains out.   And
when he finally got ready to leave, and Odile was
begging him to stay a little longer, he remembered
Hertha's words: was he just a miserable philistine,
after all?   A store clerk who would salute a pile of
shit?

He borrowed thirty francs from Odile and left her
his address.   He'd never mentioned Hertha.

At that time, he worked in the shipping department
of a brass pipe wholesaler.   Soon after his vacation,
they hired a new guy, one that he knew from the
pen.   Rudger Kanold, a harmless scatterbrain who'd
been caught stealing a few marks while reading gas
meters in people's homes.   They both wondered why
their boss hired a hunchback secretary, old people,
and ex-con's like himself and Rudger.   The whole
company was crawling with sad cases who all had
their pants full of shit for fear of losing their jobs.
He christened their outfit: Fearful & Co.   Not a
single soul was in the union and nobody knew
anything about minimum wages.   And everybody
ready and eager to do the boss a favor after quitting
time—for a hand-out or a friendly handshake.

Hertha wrote him from Cannes that she was ready
to come back.   But she stayed another nine weeks.
One Sunday, however, she stood in his doorway with

a bouquet of rosemary and beach thistles. He thought: What a classy woman! She smelled of sun tan oil and Mediterranean heat. Next to her tan he came off looking like a piece of white cheese. The poet had visited her in Cannes, but only for five days. After that, she'd thrown him out. Now the poet had given her notice to move out at her earliest convenience and Claus suggested that she move in with him. For the time being at least. It's crazy, after all, to look for a place without giving yourself enough time. He thought that he had acted rather boldly, and was taken by surprise when she accepted his offer.

That night he got plastered, not sure whether it was because of shock or happiness.

Hertha moved in the next day with two suitcases and a typewriter. She took all his centerfolds off the walls and replaced them with an original Russian ikon and a drawing by Horst Janssen. She also had a telephone installed. For a few seconds an ugly thought shot through Claus's head: Is she really as classy as I first thought she was? Does she have to take refuge with me?

She went through his closet and discovered his Sunday clothes: a navy blue suit, shiny tie and black shoes with pointed toes. She said: You can't be serious! She threw them into the hallway. He swallowed hard and dumped them in the garbage can without protesting. She put up a battery of spice racks in the kitchen and announced that she was going to design a program of culture and education for him.

Until then he'd never been to the theatre. He
doesn't want to go so far as saying that the theatre
bores him, but it really isn't his idea of a good time.
Those chic women all over the place! Even when
Hertha said a theatre was left-wing, he seemed to be
surrounded by the same bullshit and overdressed
broads. And it finally got through to him that you
weren't supposed to look for suspense, but for
content, message and the name of the director. That
way, one could compare things.

Every night they ran all over Berlin until twelve or
one in the morning. Every so often they would run
into old friends of Hertha's. Sometimes he felt like
joining their conversations, but from the faces that
Hertha made he gathered that it might be better if
he kept his mouth shut for the time being, even
though some of them encouraged him to talk. He
had some especially open and natural conversations
with Alma, the poet's ex-wife, who was now living
with an artist. But Hertha said: Be quiet! They
just want to see a monkey dance. He, however,
hadn't had that feeling at all.

They talked all night at home, rarely going to bed
before three o'clock. But he had to be up at
six—usually with a head like a rattling bucket.
Hertha did make him coffee and, when they
overslept, she would drive him to work. But she
could always crawl back in the sack and get some
more sleep. And after that, she could go swimming.
At night she was ready to spring into action, while
he was too beat to do anything but fall into bed.
Sometimes he went on strike and just fell asleep.
But then Hertha would say: What a wimp! and go
out by herself. This didn't make him any happier.

They slept through the alarm clock more and more often. His boss warned him about it twice. Then, on a day when he had called in sick again, he ran into his boss right in the middle of downtown. He was drunk and in a crazy good mood. He patted his boss on the back, and said: We're only young once! The next morning he got his pink slip.

He wasn't too upset about losing his job. The only thing that bothered him was the timing. He and Rudger had gone to the Union's main office and then began to sign up members in secret. They had been about to call their first Union meeting. Hertha hadn't been against it, but she'd said: So what? Today's unions have all bought into the system anyway, so they probably won't change anything.

It depressed him to see how easily he was brushed aside. He knows, of course, that if an old-fashioned capitalist is pushed into behaving like a modern entrepreneur, nothing much is won. He agreed with Hertha that the basic situation would probably stay the same. But he regrets not having had the experience of success he and his buddies might have had.

Unemployment gave him the chance to sleep in as long as he wanted. Hertha said that her 800 marks would get them through, but it turned out that 800 marks weren't enough, since they kept on going out, and buying expensive food and booze. At that point, Hertha decided to go to Frankfurt and try to get some more money out of her ex-husband. He didn't like the idea at first, but in the end he said: This Martin means nothing to me. If the guy really makes his money by exploiting other people, then there's nothing wrong with getting some of it for ourselves.

Hertha took off at seven in the morning. At eight, he was already lonely and scared. Bullshit, he said to himself. She'll feel the same way. But he went out to the Autobahn and started to hitch to Frankfurt. He got there at six. Hertha had given him her friend's phone number where she thought she may be staying. A man answered when he called, and then Hertha came to the phone, sounding to him as if she were in a very good mood. No, he shouldn't worry, everything is just fine. She's about to go to Martin's to squeeze him for some more dough.

He hadn't told her he was in Frankfurt.

He found Martin's address in the phone book, a nice neighborhood with villas and lots of trees. A party was going on in the garden, and the smell of broiling steaks was wafting from the grill. In the dark, he jumped over the fence and took cover behind some bushes. He really didn't know what the hell got into him. It was clear, though, that if someone found him there he would really be in deep shit. He crouched in the bushes in a cold sweat and stared at the people, twenty or thirty in all, most of them unrecognizable because of the dim lights. Some sat or stood around the grill. Hertha was squatting on the lawn next to a burly, blonde hunk. Later, she danced with him, pressing herself tightly against the guy's body. Claus had always thought that Martin was short, fat and not at all good looking. But that didn't seem to be the case. Martin looked like the type that ran around on tennis courts. Even at fifty he'd probably look young and energetic. A girl stood beside him who could have been Hertha's younger sister. Hertha was about twice as big as she was. Hertha really looked a little clumsy among these people. At times, she just stood around by herself, as if the other guests were avoiding her, a stranger in their circle. For a few minutes he felt pity and wanted to come out and take her away. But then she proceeded to hang on the blonde hunk again, letting him touch her all over. Claus suddenly felt like taking a mallet and beating this laughing, babbling, boozing crowd into the ground.

Later on a man came close to where he was hiding and peed into the bushes. He told himself: It's time to move. Soon everyone will be ready to take a piss in the bushes because they're all too drunk and lazy to go inside to the bathroom. He beat a hasty retreat, trudging through the city for hours until he reached the Autobahn.

Hertha came back in a week—tired and in a bad mood. He joked: Your stud in Frankfurt must really be something else if you're that tired. Hertha's reply was aggressive. She said that she could do with her body whatever she pleased and that he had better not bother her with his dirty-minded fantasies. She had other things to worry about anyway. Martin wanted to marry again, and he only wanted to pay her for another six months. Martin, that asshole, had suggested that she look for work.

At first he was floored by how readily she admitted cheating on him. But then he felt much better when he realized that without her alimony she was worth just as much as he was. It's finally her turn! He

said that she ought to start working right away.
What does she have a typewriter for? Hertha
complained that all newspapers that paid were
either revisionist or reactionary. That was just too
much for him. Who the hell is paying his wages? Is
he working for a socialist corporation? Isn't he
forced to sell his labor power to whoever pays the
most for it? Does he have the right to inquire into
the political preferences of his boss?

He found a student who needed his thesis typed.
After ten pages, the student took his manuscript
back—too many typos, too sloppy. Hertha yelled at
the top of her lungs that she was no fucking
secretary! She had always used the two-finger
system for her own articles.

They noticed a billboard: The Red Cross is looking
for women to take a course in nursing! How about
that? he asked. Does she have ideological qualms
about this one, too?

Hertha signed up. For the first time, they both
had to get up early in the morning. He'd gotten a
job in a shipping department again—sanitary
installations. In the evening, Hertha studied her
booklet of nursing terms: sputum, corcium,
decubitus, etc. She constantly threw up. After her
first day as an aide she came home white as
bleached flour. She had trouble breathing and never
wanted to go back to the hospital again. In the
morning, she had been assigned to take care of the
spittoons and bed pans on the geriatric ward. She
had to stir the contents and look for blood. Then she
had to empty and wash them. At noon, a young RN
handed her a cancerous breast in a dish and asked

her to bring the cadaver to the doctor on the next floor.

Hertha pulled herself together and ran up and down the hallways, emptying pans, wiping asses, making beds, cleaning sores, brushing loose teeth, cutting nails and massaging old backs with rubbing alcohol. Claus thought, full of admiration: She's a classy woman, after all!

But then somebody called her from Munich at one-thirty in the morning: Hertha is needed as an assistant director on a movie set on the Island of Sylt.   Hertha   cried   and   covered   Claus   with kisses — that's how happy she felt. She dumped her internship immediately and took off.

Five days later she was back, grouchy and subdued. The whole New Wave in movie making is nothing but the emperor's new clothes, she announced. He found a contract in her purse. Under the heading of "employed as" was the title "script girl." It seemed that she hadn't managed that one too well.

After that, she sat in front of the tube for days on end.   She didn't do any shopping or cleaning, got drunk early every night and didn't want to be touched.   Once, he asked her in a low voice if he should feed her and wipe her ass?

Then he received a telegram from Odile in Dresden: Will arrive on Monday, four o'clock, Friedrichstrasse Station!   He told Hertha that he had stayed at Odile's and how her family had been so hospitable to him, and that he would really appreciate it if Hertha would go somewhere else for a few days. He, after all, can also do what he pleases with his body.

Hertha threw some clothes in a suitcase and headed for Alma's.   He went grocery shopping and then cooked up a storm for Odile: scrambled eggs with chives, steak on toast with pineapple, orange salad and camembert.   Then he and Odile hit the sack. He'd just begun his second round when Hertha called — she'd be at the door in ten minutes to talk to him.   He apologized to Odile: He isn't, of course, single anymore and has to take care of his old lady now.

Hertha drove him to Alma's.   He managed a third round.   Hertha was as soft and sweet as she had not been for a long time.   Afterwards, she wanted to know how he felt.   Great, he said, really wonderful! She sneered: He'd never felt so successful, had he? Loading toilet bowls during the day and playing Don Juan at night.   That's exactly how insipid she always thought philistine sex to be — when his dick is up, a man stands tall, no matter how crooked he lies.

He could have busted her in the chops.   But he controlled himself and thought about what she said. And in the end, he thought: This woman really does have class!

So now he stopped fooling around with other women. He really has to develop his mind if he wants to be more than Hertha's "primitive."   Yesterday, for example, they went to a wedding.   Alma married her artist.   Her father is a big shot in a Dusseldorf mustard factory and he rented a banquet hall and arranged for a royal dinner: piles of flowers, real silver candle holders and four crystal goblets at each place setting.   Everyone thought that it was a bit overdone, but they kept quiet so as not to spoil the old man's good mood. Alma had begged them to stay cool — she'd hoped that to top off the wedding, her father would present her with a check for a new car. But "The Father of the Bride," as he referred to himself, only made a speech, and in order to acquaint the guests with one another, he said something nice about each person at the table.

When he got to Claus, he said: This is a working man, a man who creates with his hands. Nowadays, no one is surprised to find someone like himself in our circle. Times, thank God, have changed. Youth has recognized equality earlier than the older generation and has allied itself with those whose hard work lay the foundation for our common progress and prosperity! Then he paused and looked over the group as if he wanted their special attention. For this reason, he continued, the working man is to be especially welcomed in this circle of Art, Intellect and Industry.

Claus turned to Hertha and said: This old asshole needs his nigger. Otherwise he won't feel white enough. But this really isn't the place to settle up with his type. Hertha kissed him and told him that she really loved him when he was so reasonable and self-confident. He thought: I could stay with this woman forever. We have a real meeting of the minds.

Shortly after midnight the whole gang moved to a regular bar, without the old folks. When he and Hertha walked in, everybody shouted: Aha, Hertha's here! Hertha has arrived! He said to himself: What the hell is this? It sounds like they've all been to bed with her, like she's the center of the universe! He sat down somewhere, drumming his fingers on the table, and he felt like breaking every guy's neck who'd shouted: Hertha's here! He got good and drunk, staggered out the door, stood outside in the cold for fifteen minutes, went back in and demanded that Hertha drive him home.

They did make up the same night. So why is he sitting here in his regular bar now, anyway, getting loaded and talking his head off? Why is he putting off going to bed with her?

Today she was in a really good mood. She had been accepted for enrollment in the Academy for Social Work without her bachelor's degree and, as a divorcee, was even entitled to a scholarship. He doesn't quite trust the whole thing and he isn't sure that she'll be able to follow through with it. But still, in three or four years she may be something after all. And himself?

He'd felt better when he was still roaming the city streets with a buddy, ripping off parked cars. They'd really cleaned up: cameras, portable radios, purses. He isn't afraid of going to jail again. That's not the reason he stays clear of that business. But if he doesn't get his ass in gear pretty soon, he'll really look pretty low next to Hertha. That's why he's taking an Open University course in Historical and Dialectical Materialism. He's already gone to two sessions. There were some nice girls in the class but they looked as if they had missed some sleep and he thought: Boy, they really must have fucked a lot last night! But then they reported that they had been putting up posters and distributing leaflets.

That really impressed him. He also wants to work with a group. He wants people to shout: Claus is here! Claus has arrived! He's in no position to enroll in an Acadamy the way Hertha can. In this society he hasn't got that option. This society is made for people like her, no matter how much she denies it, and it was Hertha who taught him that, even if she herself doesn't understand it. He finds it funny how undialectical she is in this respect. But he's also afraid that if he learns how to take a closer look at this society, it's possible that he may end up looking at Hertha with different eyes as well.

Today he could kick himself for not tearing into that "Father of the Bride" last night. That hypocritical windbag had used him as a liberal alibi. He should have thrown his dinner in the man's face — decorated his bald head with smoked salmon. He should have asked Alma and all the others who were into that fashionable bar scene, how come they sound so revolutionary during demonstrations but become instantly smooth and docile when a paying dad is running the show. He remembers the night when Hertha smashed the wine bottle against the wall in her ex-husband's house. Why hadn't she been so courageous last night? Is it because it's bad manners to shock an old man who can't be blamed for being a reactionary, on an occasion like that? Hertha would probably argue more elegantly. She would quote Rosa Luxemburg: Individual anarchistic actions are reckonings without one's host. But who says that he wants to reckon with his host?

He will have to learn a lot now. He only hopes that he'll remember that tomorrow when he's sober again.

PAYDAY

Johannes died on Sunday night. They probably could have fixed his broken pelvis and maybe even the punctured lung where his ribs went through; but the splinters in his brain (he took a header into a woodpile) — those splinters did him in. Luckily, he never came out of the coma. His death is really getting at me.

At the hospital, I wanted to give Rita a hug, but she screamed at me and spit in my face. You rotten bastard, she said, it's all your fault!

It isn't true. It's not fair. So I just left her standing there. I'm sure she'll quiet down and get over it eventually. She's still young. One day I'll explain everything to her and then she'll understand. Johannes had only himself to blame.

That first Friday, we told ourselves: It's the guy's first week on the job and he probably needs all the cash. So, we let him go. We'll wait till next payday. But next Friday his wife shows up right after the first break and takes the whole packet home with her.

Our foreman mumbles something nasty into his sandwich, but Johannes isn't even listening. I buy some beer for myself, the foreman and the other three bricklayers. I pretend that I'm going to offer one to Johannes — he just shakes his head and pours another coffee from his Thermos. I joke around: Alcohol is really bad news on the job; milk is so much better!

Johannes doesn't even get the drift. Yes, he says, totally innocent, I drink milk every morning.

And that's how he is: he's bigger and taller than I am, but his face looks like a bowl of oatmeal. I swear that next week he won't get away. He'll have to pay up. So when he shows up at work the next morning and says, hi, I look at him and say: Today, Johannes, today is Friday.

Yeah, he says, great! Tomorrow's Saturday and then we'll be done with another week.

The pig-headed bastard! In a way, I like it though, and I think: That guy knows what he wants. But it still pisses me off.

He changes his clothes in the shed and it always seems to take an eternity since he dresses like he worked in an office. He doesn't just hang his shirt and tie on a nail, he arranges everything neatly on a coat hanger. Then he waits at the scaffold elevator for me to bring him bricks and mortar. I want to start a conversation, so I roll the wheelbarrow over his foot.

He curses. He tells me to watch it.

I shrug it off. I'm superstitious, Johannes, I say. This kind of thing always happens to guys like you. I once knew a guy who didn't pay up for his share of the footing. He always said that only nuts pay for their footing. Well, one day a bucket of water falls on his head and he's knocked off the scaffold. After he comes back from the hospital, a beam hits him in the back and wrecks his spine. How much do you think he'd give today to have paid his footing? But instead he's on skid row, picking cigarette butts out of the gutter.

Johannes yells after me: What do you mean by that?

When I come around with my next load he tells me that scare tactics won't work on him.

The thing is — I really am superstitious.

At ten-thirty the messenger comes from the company office. The foreman calls us in one at a time and gives us our pay envelopes. When I step out of the trailer I see Rita waiting on the sidewalk, but I don't see Johannes anywhere. I run around the building to the john and knock on the door — I know he's hiding in there. He follows me to the elevator, buttoning his pants on the way. He runs my wheelbarrow up.

Anything wrong? he yells down to the sidewalk.

His wife just shakes her head in wonder and waits. Johannes leans on the brake lever, acting as if he had to stay up there all day.

Then she suddenly comes over and stands next to us, holding her shopping bag in front of her legs and looking confused. What's the matter? she asks.

I take a good look at her for the first time. She doesn't have much under her blouse, but her legs look nice. Her head is small and narrow, and her eyes are kind of big. I know the type: they keep their apartments in top shape, always have some flowers in the window box and a few beers in the fridge. On weekends they sometimes have a little booze and they aren't all that bad in bed.

Don't get into a fight, I say, and move away with a load of bricks. Rita talks to Johannes. He shuffles like a coward and looks around to see if anyone's watching. He finally pulls his pay envelope out of his pocket and gives her four bills. I think: That can't be all! And sure enough, she keeps at him, but in a low voice so I couldn't catch a single word, until Johannes digs into his pockets again.

I have to admire his fortitude, but it doesn't seem to make him too happy. He bores the tip of his shoe into the ground and scratches his ass so often I want to ask him if he's got the piles.

He says that this month is particularly tight since they bought a new bed. It's not that he wants to weasel out of anything, but he wonders if maybe the guys have forgotten about the footing by now?

All I can tell him is that my memory is very fresh. I don't know about the others, and I don't care either. All he has to do as far as I'm concerned is buy me a beer after work.

Alright, he says. One beer won't kill me. He tries to put a fifty-pfennig piece into my hand.

I ask him if he's gone nuts. Hell, I say, If you want to buy me a beer you'll have to come down to the bar after work!

When I finally get him this far, I almost feel like going by myself. I'd never been more disgusted with anyone in my life.

The bar where I hang out on Friday nights isn't far from the construction site—just a few blocks. The clientele are usually other hard hats, streetcar conductors (the depot is across the street), some guineas, and a few bums. I have a regular table.

On the way, I ask him: Johannes, you never go for a beer, do you?

Not often, he says. We usually have a good time at home. You can do all kinds of things at home.

What things?

Well, work on the apartment and stuff like that. He says that he'd really like to have a little house, considering he works construction, but that's a dream for now. But he likes to keep the apartment in good shape. Soon he'll be able to buy a used car so they can take rides in the country once in a while.

And you never cheat on your wife? I ask. He pretends he doesn't even know that that kind of thing goes on. Hell, I say, marriage gets a man down. I couldn't stand a life like that. And I tell him about the two years I worked in Holland and the year I spent in Switzerland. I also tell him that I've been in England and Denmark and that during all that time I never saved a penny. I say: What I need I always get, and I'm the kind of guy who needs another woman every week-end. As long as you're young you have to have some adventure, don't you think?

What adventure? he asks. Anyway, he says, one of these days he's going to take a trip abroad. Maybe a

camping trip to Italy next summer. Whatever,
different strokes for different folks. What's most
important to him, in the end, is that we all
understand each other as human beings.

What on earth can you say to stuff like that? All I
can do is shake my head.

The bar is packed from the counter to the door. The
guys are playing cards at the tables. A march is
blaring from the juke box and Joseph, the old bum,
stands in front of it, conducting. That guy will
waste his last dime on a march. He tells anyone
who'll listen that when he was a corporal in the
Ukraine, he killed 800 Russians in one afternoon.

The guy is nuts, I tell Johannes, so he'll pass Joseph
by. He's never been in the army. The way he looks,
I bet he's done time in a concentration camp.

We work our way back to the corner table. The
corner smells a little on account of being so close to
the mens room, but at least you can sit there
without being bothered by anyone. Karl and Heini
are already there. Heini, as usual, is busy folding
paper dolls out of newspaper. If those damned dolls
were worth a penny a piece, he'd be a millionaire by
now.

Karl puts out his left hand to shake. He used to be
an amateur boxing champion, and he worked on the
railroad until his arm got caught between two
buffers. I know Karl's trick: he grabs a guys fingers
and squeezes them till he screams and says uncle.
Johannes doesn't say uncle, though. He just smiles
an embarrassed smile.

Heini just nods hello. He'll be finished in a second, he says. Heini's a streetcar conductor, and collects porno photos. His paper dolls always have something to do with sex.

Gerda comes over before we even have a chance to pull our chairs out from under the table. I've never seen another waitress who'll go along with as many jokes as Gerda. Once in a while I take her home with me. She's so well-rounded that you don't have to put a pillow under her. I grab her ass and tell Johannes: Pinch this and you'll really have something in your hands!

At first Gerda wants to play coy and she gives me a light slap in the face. But when she sees how quickly our 'oatmeal face' backs into the farthest corner, she asks: Where the hell did you pick that one up? Maybe the giant baby is still a virgin? But she says, Oh dear! when she notices that Johannes hardly knows where to look.

I order beer and schnapps for us. Heini shows his latest paper doll around. We all pull at the back of the doll's coat and laugh when its dick comes out the front.

Listen, kids! Today in the streetcar . . . (Heini's streetcar stories are always real classics): there's this guy standing on the car platform, and I see him slowly backing into a girl. When these guys get that look on their face, I already know why their hands are hanging down. The car comes to a stop. When it starts again, an old lady's standing behind the guy, but he doesn't notice and he keeps his hands busy behind him. And the old lady keeps still, doesn't make a sound, but her mouth looks as if she's about to smack her lips. All of a sudden the guy sees his girl over by the door. He looks behind him and is really shocked. He moves away fast—right across the car. I go after him and ask him whether he's already payed me. Boy, you should've seen how hard that guy rummaged through his pockets to find the ticket!

Karl says that guys like that are disgusting. He says that if he ever catches one of them, he'll dangle him out the window by a finger; from the tenth floor! His finger, he boasts, can hold two thousand pounds!

Johannes says, Oh! but in a doubtful rather than amazed way. Karl challenges him: Show me your hand. They put their elbows on the table and start to arm wrestle. Karl laughs: Everybody watch this!

So far, Karl's always won. Lately, he even has trouble finding new challengers. There are certain customers who secretly work out, hoping to defeat him someday, so once in a while a guy will come in and announce that today's the day! The last one came in two or three months ago and Karl's starting to mumble something about changing his hang-out.

Heini's bored. He starts making a new doll. I order another beer.

After a minute or two, both arms are still up. Heini interrupts his project and watches. I look at my watch and start to count the seconds. Gerda's leaning against my chair, pressing her hip against my shoulder. Karl's face gets puffy and red, and keeps on swelling with effort and rage. People are starting to notice and they crowd in around the table, goading Karl on. Some start mocking: If you lose, you'll have to buy the house a round! Or: Hey, Karl! You've met your match. It's all down hill from here! And I keep counting: Fifty-seven, fifty-eight, fifty-nine . . .

After he's won, Johannes says: I used to wrestle. It sounds like an apology. I'm amazed that there's so much strength in the oatmeal face! Karl says: Well, wrestlers . . . He pulls his head away when Gerda strokes his hair and says in a comforting voice: Wash it down . . .

Karl pays for a round. I bet there's never been a round that's made him more miserable than this one. Gerda notices it. She's a really good waitress. She tells him: Karl, show us that trick with your tongue.

That trick is Karl's big performance. He can stick out his tongue and turn it upside down like a hand, letting all the reddish muscles and blue veins underneath it hang out. He does it over and over again till his tongue hurts. Johannes watches him open-mouthed. He tries to do it with his own tongue, but behind his hand so no one notices. I can see it because I'm facing him, but he can't quite make it. He just looks like an idiot.

Then Johannes looks at his watch and says: I've got to go now. Nothing against you guys, but I've got to get home and paint the pipes under the sink. And I think: Now, he'll just go and leave us sitting here. But he doesn't. He just sits there, looking around sheepishly.

I realize that he just doesn't fit in. Karl, of course, would rather that he did leave, but Johannes has been drinking with us and still hasn't bought a single round. That really gets me. When I remind him, he pretends he's forgotten all about it. He's sorry, he says, and he asks whether he can pay for the round I'd just ordered. It's already been paid for, I tell him, so you have to stay and order one for yourself.

He quickly orders some more drinks, and then asks if it's alright if he stays for another half-hour. We just crack up! I can see that Karl is just dying to tell him what an asshole he is, but anyone who pays is always welcome with us.

Next, Karl sniffs a piece of string up his nose and spits it out of his mouth. He also bites a piece off a saucer. For my part, I put out a cigarette in the palm of my hand — it's not as bad as it looks. Heini shows us some new card tricks. Johannes is the only one who dredges up the old numbers: putting the wrong end of his cigarette in his mouth, turning up his eye-lids, and flipping the cardboard coasters and catching them before they hit the table.

We've put away a hell of a lot of beer and schnapps, and Johannes finally loosens up a little. When he goes to take a leak, he has to hold himself up. But Heini's story about the hooker who can pick up coins with her snatch puts Johannes over the edge. This hooker was picking up the coins off the edge of a chair, Heini says, so I heated up a five-mark piece with my lighter and put it down. Boy, he says, You should've seen her dance!

Johannes pounds the table, while we laugh at him. He slaps Heini on the shoulder and calls him an old sunnuvabitch. I've never had this much fun in my whole life, he says to me. Really! He's gotten to know some swell guys here, he says. And the party's a smashing success. He yells for Gerda to bring a round of double schnapps. Gerda looks at him as if she hadn't heard right. You heard him, I tell her.

How'd you guys like it if I stand on my hands? says Johannes. I've done it before — even on chimneys!

Karl starts heckling: You're bragging! You'll never do it! and Gerda says that there's a dye-shop with a chimney in the yard behind the bar. There are even rungs on the chimney so you can climb it. Then she suddenly starts acting real horny: I'll give you a kiss, she tells him. Afterwards, of course.

But Johannes wants the kiss right away. He pulls her over by her arm, puts her on his lap, grabs her by the neck, and starts kissing her like a maniac, rummaging under her skirt with his other hand. Gerda makes some muffled noises and tries to cover her bare legs with the tablecloth. Heini narrows his eyes and moves closer. Gerda slaps his hand. When she gets her mouth free, she bawls him out: Isn't one man at a time enough?

I don't know who notices Rita first. She's standing two feet away from us, looking at her husband as if she were watching a horror movie. We all duck for a minute because we expect some screaming, but when nothing happens the tension relaxes. We laugh, 'cause Johannes face is something else!

You'd better cover your ass, Karl tells him, 'cause you've got it coming!

But Rita just looks like she's whipped. I'm sure that it's the first time she's ever had to comb the bars looking for her husband.

Johannes gets rowdy. He yells at her: Get out! Get the hell out of here! Scram! Go home! It's Friday night and I finally want to do what I like. I don't need no goddamn peeper following me around.

Gerda wants to sneak away, but she forgets the hand between her thighs. Her skirt slides up and everybody can see her panties. She tries to jerk Johannes hand away and punches his shoulder.

Sit down! he tells her and puts her back on his lap. Then he screams at Rita some more: Out, I said! And he points to the door with his free hand. Rita's face splotches red and she turns and runs to the exit.

Where's that chimney? asks Johannes.

Heini and Karl, who are also pretty loaded, lead him behind the counter and out into the yard. A few people follow them. I stay. I assume, of course, that they won't let him even close to the chimney. They must know that Johannes is in no shape to climb at all. How could I know that he actually made it up twenty rungs?

So I stay calm. I don't expect anything bad to happen. Otherwise, I would have tried to stop it, naturally.

I think: Take a look at how the woman is doing. She can't be too far away. I admit that I have a weakness for women with husband trouble. I have some experience with that.

She's standing on the sidewalk in front of the bar as if it were a bus stop. Some drunk has already propositioned her and she's crying hard, so I tell her: Come on girl, we're going to have a drink.

She nods, and I put my arm around her. I lead her away and we find another bar. I order some whiskey and I talk to her: Listen, I say, we're still young and we have to be forgiving; and something different once in a while certainly can't hurt.

Rita just keeps shaking her head, dries her tears with my handkerchief, and says: No, I can't believe that Johannes would do anything like that.

I say: Everybody does.

She drinks a lot, and very fast. More than she can hold. Suddenly she puts her head on my shoulder. Then she feels sick and says that she'd like to lie down for a while.

I settle up. It's not far to my place. I offer to let her lie down and rest for an hour or so. I'm not sure if she understands what I want right away. At first I think: This is going to be a scene! But then everything goes nice and smooth. And after a while, I even begin to enjoy it, though she still keeps on crying.

CLARIFICATIONS

He wants to make it perfectly clear that he doesn't depend on anybody. He stands on his own two feet. He's known where it's at since he was twelve years old and maybe you want to hear his story.

For instance, he asks his old man for money, but his old man says he's gotta be out of his mind. Alright, so he won't get an allowance. So what does he do? He gets a job at the amusement park after school, collecting ticket money for the merry-go-round and the bumper cars. They always need a fast hand. The quicker he is, the better the boss likes it since he always likes to short the rides when they're real busy. Of course he isn't just working for the boss. After all, he's got his own pockets to fill. He gets an idea. He buys a brass ring and solders on a fifty-pfennig piece. Then he puts on the ring so the coin is inside the palm of his hand, okay? Now, when a customer gives him a five-mark piece, he pulls the change out of his pocket, holding it around the coin on the ring — all very smooth and not too quick. The customer counts the change along with him, opens his hand or wallet to take it and is satisfied. Nobody counts a second time. Nobody ever misses the soldered coin. Why should they? After all, they've counted their money. This scam gets him three or four marks every day.

On graduation day, the school principal makes his speech: Only men with ideas will make it in the world! Only this kind of man will rise above the masses! That kind of shit just makes him yawn; he's already bought a moped with his savings.

His old man wants to get him into the factory; into
an apprenticeship program. But he's not stupid.
Punch a time-clock every morning and every night?
Polish machinery? Get lunch and beer for the
foreman? Not him! He wants to be independent, to
stay a free man.

He starts off shoveling coal and stacking briquettes
in his neighbors' basements. He hauls the coal
upstairs for the old ladies and splits their firewood.
He's done this kind of work since he was eight years
old and he knows his stuff. The people appreciate
his work and they pay well. Every once in a while
he picks up junk he can sell; wine bottles, scrap
metal, a bike cover or an old radio.

His old man tells him that it's no way to make a
living—that you don't make the right contacts in
that line of work.

The old man doesn't know what he's talking about.
He's already got friends, friends that go to good
schools—at least since he got to know Monika.

He's only sixteen but he looks like eighteen, so he
gets this job taking care of the heating system for a
big nursery in North Berlin. His furnace controls
the temperature of all the greenhouses. If he messes
up by just a few centigrades, all the plants will be
ruined, but he knows his heating—and he's on the
boss's good side. And then there's Monika, who also
works at the nursery. Monika: a fat white mouse.
The only thing missing is red eyes. A real bimbo.
You can hear her giggling all the time. Sometimes
during lunch hour she hangs around the boiler room
like a moron, asking: What color do you think my

underwear is? When he wants to look, she scratches him. She has wicked fingernails. She doesn't do that for too long though — he has her tamed in about a month. She tags along after him without a leash. But sometimes she keels over. Just like that. Wham — she just lies there, her eyes all rolled up with the whites showing. Epilepsy. It's really funny.

His buddies like it when he brings her along. Monika will do anything if you pump enough beer into her.

He knows where there's this shack in the Tegel Woods. Most of the time there's hay in it. That's where they go with their five or six mopeds; Monika riding with one of the guys, drunk and giggling. The boys hide their portable record player and flashlights in the hay. Monika dances with all of them and doesn't really care who undresses her. The only trouble spot is her bra. She doesn't like to let it go because she says she can't dance with it off. She's something else! The ultimate bimbo.

In court, she names eleven guys who could be the father. Even the judge tells her to go home, make some kind of first choice, and then come back — if she still has the guts to do it. It's her own fault. Why doesn't she take precautions? As far as he's concerned, he's always said: Look out for number one! For instance, that strike at the nursery.

He's got to say that the boss is a real pig. The guy's always bitching that the vegetables are rotting, the flowers are wilting, things have to be shipped out right away. He makes them work overtime, but he doesn't want to pay them for it. Anyway, he himself thinks striking is dumb. He doesn't join; why should he pull someone else's chestnuts out of the fire? Besides, he can't just let the furnace and greenhouses go cold. During the strike week he works for five and gets paid for ten. The boss's son even lets him drive the delivery van, though he doesn't have a driver's license. He makes a real bundle that week.

But then he's also glad that a few months later the boss put in an automatic heating system and had to let him go. The other workers didn't like him too much anyway. So he's free again. He can look for a new job any time he wants to. And he makes friends; as many as he likes and whenever he wants to — even rich ones. Maybe he never would've made friends with Herbert if he hadn't been out of work.

Herbert's parents own a supermarket in Bremen and he's finishing his apprenticeship in his uncle's store here. Herbert is a wild guy. For instance, he has the hots for Marlene, who's parents own a cigar store across the street. Marlene goes to a good school and she doesn't look too bad either. She's blonde and stuff. But she keeps on turning Herbert down. Herbert acts like he's got an ulcer. He picks her up twice a week after her violin lessons and he wants to carry the case, but she won't let him. At night Herbert stands at her door, rings the bell and whistles, but Marlene doesn't show.

To be honest, he thinks that her stuck-up act stinks. He'd tell her to piss off, but Herbert hangs in there and this impresses him.

One night Herbert says that if anyone can tell him how he can get to make it with Marlene, he'll give them a hundred marks. All the guys start talking at the same time but they all finally come up empty. Again, he gets another solid idea—he cooks up a plan that he's proud of to this day. Not just Herbert, but the whole gang should put the move on Marlene. They'll all go after her, get on her nerves until she's had it up to her eyeballs and runs to Herbert for protection. He's the one she'll be grateful to for keeping the flies off of her. Some plan, right?

Exactly thirty-eight days later he's working for Herbert's uncle. He drives a Mercedes van and is on the road all day long. A great job: he makes deliveries, talks a lot to all kinds of people, gets a lot of tips, picks up stock at the railroad station, the wholesale market and, also, at his old nursery. Monika is still there. She turns green when she sees him—the white mouse is still a flaming bitch. But when he offers her a ride home, she climbs into the Mercedes. When he puts his hand up her skirt she makes a face, but doesn't do anything else except look out the window. Damned broads!

His plan works. He successfully delivers Marlene into Herbert's hands, but now Herbert wants to get rid of her! No problem. He picks her up at school and asks her, for instance: How did you like the movie last night? What do you mean? she says, I didn't go to the movies! Like hell you didn't go to the movies, he'd say. Herbert himself told me that he took his girlfriend to the movies last night! Then he acts like he let the cat out of the bag by accident and he tells her not to take it too seriously.

He makes up stories like these for a whole month. Herbert, of course, denies everything. That's part of the plan. Finally, he asks Marlene if she's pregnant. He tells her that Herbert knocks up all the girls he goes to bed with—it's kind of a game with him. At that point she's had enough. She quits. He and Herbert laugh their heads off.

Yeah, he's had a good time with Herbert. Herbert calls him a 'hauler.' He always says: Hey, hauler, haul in some ass! When it comes to hauling in women, he can't be beat and that's no lie. If there's some broad he likes, he just taps her on the shoulder and says: Hi, kid. How about some champagne? They always like champagne. Particularly the real young teenagers. That's why he thinks it's kind of shabby when Herbert gets rid of him the night the Mercedes gets broken into and cleaned out. That can happen to anyone. It was late and he'd parked the van at his place. Herbert claims that he broke into the van himself, but that's crazy! If he wants to steal something, he has better ways of doing it. But you can't win 'em all. It's not so bad having to look for something new every few years. He always has new ideas. Not like his old man, hanging around the factory all his life and proud of it.

And now, guess what he started next? You'll never guess! Tell you in a minute, but first, this is how he gets to know Barbara.

He's been out of work for a while and he's just goofing off. Sometimes he helps out at a gas station and once in a while he gets called for part-time work at the Post Office. He doesn't think you need to work all the time and, anyway, he still has a couple of bucks in the bank. One day he's hanging around the hot-dog stand under the Beusselstrasse El, nursing a coke, when this guy pushes past him to get to the counter. He starts telling the woman that he bought a pack of cigarettes earlier in the day and payed with a two-mark piece, but, because his train was coming, he ran for it and forgot his change. He had to come back, he said, because he's a college student and he needs every mark he can get.

The woman can't remember, but the guy looks like he's just about to cry, so she gives him the money. Honestly, the student looks kind of suspicious to him, but he doesn't like college kids anyway. They have a weird way of looking at people. But, what the hell!

He gets on the same train with the student. He has to change at the next station, but when he gets off he sees the student get off too and head for the station hot-dog stand. He figures something's fishy here, so he follows him, just in time to hear the end of the same 'forgotten change' story. The girl behind the counter is just about to give the guy the 'change' when he lets him have it. All of a sudden there must be at least two dozen people around, amazed when he tells them about this guys' scam. One even asks him if he's a detective! They all jump on the student, but the guy manages to get away before the cops show up.

Well, eventually he moves on, but something's bothering him and he can't figure out what it is. He thinks and thinks till he's almost going crazy and all of a sudden it hits him: the girl! The girl behind the counter. She was gorgeous. She'd even thanked him — why hadn't he talked to her? Sometimes he can be a real ass! So he goes back and sees that she's not only gorgeous, she's superb!

He's been married to her for quite a few years. Her name is Barbara and she's two and a half years older than he is, but when they first met he had a hard time getting her to even go for a walk. They only got really close after he got the idea about the bar.

In those days he had that room in Spandau, right? He usually takes the bus downtown but sometimes he'd walk a stretch. He's walked past the construction site lots of times but it took him a few weeks to get the idea. He notices an apprentice hauling beer on a bicycle and remembers seeing him before — also hauling beer. He starts looking around: three high-rises, rows of apartment buildings and a laundromat in the center of the complex.

He talks to the foreman, who tells him that the project will take at least three years to complete.

And there're no beer joints around?

No, beer joints and stores are all pretty far away.

That was the moment he knew what he had to do.

The construction site borders on a woods and a few garden plots; ten or twelve lots, surrounded by fruit trees, bushes and a fence. There are also a few sheds; some painted red or blue, others falling apart. The last lot to the left looks particularly deserted — nobody's weeded it for a long time. A girl pulling weeds in another lot tells him that the owner lives in Neukolln, so he goes to see him right away.

The guy's wife has just died and he can't hardly move; he just sits in this dark stuffy room, smoking and whining. So right away he tells the old man that he'll bring him fresh fruit and vegetables, paint his room and Barbara will drop by once a week to clean, do the laundry and whatever else he needs. All he wants in return is the garden plot. The old geezer, mighty pleased, takes the offer, thinking that now he has two kids who'll take care of him.

But he and Barbara have better things to do. He has to fix up the shed, put on an addition and buy some used tables and chairs. Barbara takes care of the license, deals with City Hall and contacts the breweries. She knows she's really good at that kind of thing. She has very clear, light-grey eyes and when she stands in front of one of those clerks and tells him what she wants, it doesn't take her long to get it. Barbara has character, no lie! She looks fantastic on opening day; he'll never forget it. She'd dyed her hair blond, had it done up and wore that red blouse he'd just bought her.

Now the joint is always packed and Barbara really knows how to handle the guys. It's a pleasure to watch her work. When some guy wants to grab her legs — and she has a set of thighs that would raise the dead — she just turns on her evil eye, gives him one of her quick put-downs, and he never tries it again.

So here he is, twenty-two and he owns his own bar. That's something, right? How many other guys can say that! Now that he's got a solid base, he can get married; Barbara's going to have a baby pretty soon. After a few months she has to stay at home. She

can't stand up or run around too much in her
condition, which is too bad. But again, he has an
idea: Monika.

She still works at the nursery, but by now she's got
two kids in some foster home. He's got to fool
around with her a little before he can talk her into
coming to work at the bar but she doesn't regret it;
she really pulls in the tips. He doesn't regret it
either since the hard hats hang out at his joint even
longer than before; on weekdays as well as Fridays.
All they need is a little handy tits and ass.

Once in a while he gets scared that Monika will keel
over again; this time with a beertray in her hands,
but she says that she's on medication and can tell
ahead of time when it's going to happen. She just
goes to the bathroom till it's over. Thanks to
Monika, he can afford to put in a TV set, and once a
week he runs a Skat contest; those guys love to play
cards. Word gets around that his customers have a
good time.

Barbara likes how things are shaping up. The only
thing she doesn't like is Monika. But he
understands that women in their eighth or ninth
month always think their men cheat on them. It's
true, once in a while he stays out, but only when
he's had too much to drink. They live with their in-
laws and his father-in-law can't stand drunks, so
when he's had too many he crashes on a cot in the
bar. By himself, of course! What else? Can you
imagine two people sleeping on a cot? He can't,
anyway.

After the baby is off the bottle, Barbara goes back to work at the bar, but only until the afternoon; in the morning, she makes sandwiches for the ten o'clock break and heats up sausages for the foremen who eat lunch there. After that, she's done. She doesn't have to kill herself and the baby shouldn't be alone at night. A daughter, a darling baby, really! Anyway, Monika is better for business at night. That's something he has to think about, after all.

He makes good money for about a year and a half, so he buys a station wagon. But then he has this stupid accident. It was late again. The streetcars and buses weren't running and, as luck would have it, nobody wants to give Monika a lift that night. Out of pure decency, he gives her a ride home. Barbara, of course, says he wasn't paying attention because his hand was up Monika's skirt, as usual. Ridiculous! He had the right of way. He saw it coming and thought: I hope that American crate stops! But by that time it was all over. And, although he had the right of way, they're still saying he was reckless. That's the pits! Real assholes.

Well, Monika goes through the windshield and cuts her throat. The American car is totaled. So is his. And the insurance company won't cover it because they say he was DWI—which is also ridiculous. Bartenders always have more alcohol in their blood than other people, but nobody takes that into consideration. Now he has to pay support for Monika's kids as well as the cost of the American car—and those damned tanks cost one hell of a lot.

Fortunately, the owner of the lot died, so he can sell and cover part of his debts. He isn't shedding any tears on account of the lot and the bar. He's not the same person he used to be and really shouldn't be in that line anymore. It would have ended pretty soon anyway since construction was almost finished. They built two bars in the complex. It's true that he wanted to lease one of them, but he didn't get it. Nowadays, the Turks get all the best deals. Or certain other people . . . But he doesn't want to get into trouble by saying too much. Everyone knows what he means. And those people also get credit. Those bastards!

Barbara threw him out and she wants a divorce. She says he's become an alcoholic and ruins everything she tries to do. Also ridiculous! She'll never make that stick in court. He won't give her a divorce. For one thing, it won't be good for the kid. And for another: does she think she can leave him with all those debts! She's his wife, and is just as liable as he is. She has to pay her share. He's sure that in the end everything will be fine. He has good reason to be optimistic. He's only twenty-five. He still has a lot of time. All he has to do is wait for the right moment and be clever when it comes.

For the time being he's digging ditches. But only temporarily, though the work isn't bad; out in the woods, lots of fresh air, and stuff. And really good buddies. The foreman likes him too, and he's already told him that he's a good worker. But that doesn't mean that people can call him a 'proletarian!' That's what one of those college kids called him yesterday. He belted him one in the teeth, because he certainly isn't whatever that guy was looking for!

HIS OWN BOSS

Gerhard is out of work, but he's not particularly upset about it. After all, when does a butcher ever get a chance to sit down! He's glad to give his leg-stump a rest for a change, and leave his artificial leg standing in the corner of his room. He spends the mornings reading magazines, playing games or toys with Monika, or practicing Math and German with Brigitte, who's just made second grade and still hasn't quite gotten rid of her Saxon dialect. At noon, when Irene is cooking, he listens to what she tells him — things he had never believed before when he used to come home after work in the evening: about the cantankerous stubborness of the landlady, with whom they have to share the kitchen, her grouchy commands and her condescending remarks about Irene's way of cooking. Gerhard says: Irene is his wife, after all, whom he loves and whose best interests he has in mind. Now that he has time, he engages himself wholeheartedly on behalf of his family: he searches for new living quarters.

> DATA: Born in Berlin in 1917. His unwed mother a cleaning woman; his father a sailor who disappears to America. Moved to Freienwalde on the Oder where his grandfather lives. There, grade school and apprenticeship as a butcher. His mother is housekeeper to a retired naval officer who wants Gerhard to become a sailor.

After two weeks he finds a two-room apartment in an old brick building close to the lake in the Northeast of West Berlin. It has no indoor bathroom, to be sure, but a small garden with enough room for two lounge chairs, a few chickens and a couple of rabbit hutches. And while Gerhard is exploring his new neighborhood, having a beer here and a schnapps there, he gets to know a butcher who wants to sell his business for four thousand marks and retire. Gerhard doesn't have four thousand marks, but he takes a look at the shop anyway: the counter is clean and intact, and the storage and work rooms are properly tiled. Only the machines are too old: meatgrinder, cutter, and the bonesaw are run by a transmission belt on a single motor. Up till now the bastards have done the job, says the owner. The books, too, look alright. They show a volume of business that one could live on. Gerhard wants to pay off the purchase price over a two year period.

On opening day Gerhard puts a kidney-shaped table in one corner of the shop and decorates it with flowers. He thinks: There have to be flowers; they're part of any opening. Flowers make customers friendly. His display window, piled up with chunks of meat, is also decorated with garlands. It looks a lot more attractive than the window of his first shop in Mittwaida, during the days right after the war. He serves glasses of cold duck throughout opening day.

After a few days, however, he becomes worried. Customers only come in once in a while. They are mostly old folks who live on Social Security checks, and who want two kidneys, one small steak, tripe, a few ounces of sausage, a single slice of ham, some scrap meat for the cat, or some lung and spleen for Fido (and for free, if possible). The old-timers explain to him: more and more young people are moving into the city, or they do their shopping in the super-markets there, before coming home to the suburbs after work.

When Gerhard wants to process his first big batch of sausage, the cutter breaks down. It slows down, the belt jams and gets torn up by the flywheel. Time after time Gerhard repairs the belt, which keeps on tearing. And now he remembers: when the former owner has shown him the machines, they functioned, but without any load. Gerhard has to buy sausage because he can't produce enough of it himself. The wholesalers aren't delivering to the Northeast yet, so he has to hire a driver to bring in a pig, some mutton and a side of beef once a week. Additional expenses.

And then the septic tank backs up, water rising from the drains, and he uses a lot of water to boil meat and clean the machines. After a while he has to wear rubber boots in order to walk in his cutting room; the water covers his feet. It can't even be bailed with a bucket; it only recedes slowly on the weekends. His shop begins to smell like a sty. He wants to buy new machines, and he wants to have the septic tank cleaned, even though it's really the landlords responsibility, but the landlord is short of money. Gerhard goes to banks to inquire about loans, but he knows in advance that they won't take his hands as collateral. He'll have to throw in the towel. All he can hope for is someone with enough money to buy his business. He puts ads in all the Berlin dailies and a butcher responds. The butcher says he'll come up with enough money to haul the entire inventory to the garbage dump and put in brand new machines.   Gerhard considers himself lucky to get out breaking even.

> DATA: After his apprenticeship, without a job. Works as unskilled laborer in a quarry.   Applies to the Navy in Kiel. He scores high on his written and oral exams, and also in athletics. Because of the great number of applicants, asked to inquire again next year. Accident in the quarry: a wagon runs over one of Gerhard's legs. On the day the leg is amputated, the Navy sends notice of acceptance.

Gerhard starts working in the West Harbor for a gut importer. He manages the warehouse and controls incoming shipments as the cranes unload containers from Canada or Australia – wooden barrels full of salted cow, pig or sheep guts which have to be carefully unpacked, washed and hung up. Yards of them, filled with water, hang on wooden racks. Gerhard examines them to see whether they're torn, broken or cut anywhere. Deficient guts have to be sorted out so that they won't burst when the butchers fill them with sausage. They have to be salted again, before Gerhard can book them for further sale. They mustn't be packed too warm or too densely, so that they won't be attacked by "The Dog," a rot that can be recognized if the salt turns reddish.   Gerhard organizes a new accounting system for his boss. He knows: he's useful here; he's needed and also appreciated as a human being. When his superiors celebrate the 25th anniversary of the founding of the business and have a group photograph taken of the employees, his boss pulls him between himself and his son and puts his arm around his shoulder. That's how the picture was taken. Gerhard has the photograph enlarged and framed behind glass.

He earns enough to feed and clothe his family. Irene doesn't have to work. She and the girls take walks in the forest and along the lake, and she takes care of the household and the animals. Gerhard can now afford an old row-boat with a three horsepower motor, and this realizes, in part, a dream of his youth: to be a sailor. He cultivates an old hobby: catching carp. He's found out that the carp is a fish that can only be caught in moving waters by a very quiet and patient person — by people who are excellent observers and whose hands don't tremble. He's learned: he who goes for carp must not be discouraged by failures, must be cunning and persistent. He must be able to wait, but also grab with lightening speed. In the summer the carp emerges from the deep water around five o'clock in the morning, swims to the shallow water and follows its path between the reeds. Its presence can be recognized by the irregular movements of the reeds above the waterline, while it nibbles algae from the lower parts of the stems. Every carp has its own entrance into the reeds, its own path, and its own exit. Entrance and exit of two carp can be easily confused, because the movement of the reeds is equally strong at both. A carp will never swallow a hook at its exit, but only where it is still eager to feed.

Almost every Sunday, Gerhard can pull a carp into his boat, sometimes even two. At home, he throws them on the kitchen table and asks: Well, is this nothing?

It's something, says Irene.

On Sunday afternoons they sit in their garden or on a balcony at a friend's and kill time by playing games. Or they just shoot the breeze, as Gerhard calls it.

Then he has an accident. One of his unskilled helpers ignored his instruction, not listening to his orders. He lets a filled container slide down into the storage room where Gerhard is still trying to roll off a barrel. The container hits him on his back and head. Nothing to worry about, says the nurse when he wakes up in the hospital. Only a medium concussion, and a superficial wound that's been stitched already. An icebag lies on his head. The assistant manager brings flowers and candy the next day and sits fidgeting at his bedside, holding his hat against his belly. Don't worry, says Gerhard. In a week I'll be back on the job.

He makes it in twelve days, works diligently as before, but he notices that the running around begins to make his leg stump sore; his artificial leg is bothering him. He takes baths, massages and wraps his stump, and has the artificial leg relined. Nevertheless, in the evening he has to confess to Irene that he could cry from the pain.

> DATA: Stay in an orthopedic clinic in Berlin. Fitting of the artificial leg. Meets Irene, his later wife, who is a patient in the same clinic for a back problem.

For the first time in three years he requests a talk with his boss about a personal matter. The assistant manager sits behind the desk, his father in an easy chair to one side. Gerhard remains standing behind the chair which has been offered to him. He doesn't want to be disrespectful, doesn't want to make impossible demands. He doesn't want to harp on the fact that he had such an elevated position in the anniversary photograph. He knows how important his contribution has been to the business. He knows the things he does here, but he doesn't want to take inappropriate advantage of all this. He's not in the union, and he doesn't want to make any trouble for the boss. But he wants to ask: Wouldn't this be a good time for a little raise?

The boss is sorry. The economy is in bad shape. Investments would be necessary, but the situation forces him to cut back. He's even considering sending back some of this Turkish workers to reduce the monthly labor cost. A salary increase is, therefore, out of the question — even for the most capable employees of the firm. And the assistant manager cracks a joke: He was able to buy his new Mercedes only because he robbed his kid's piggy-bank.

Gerhard feels as if he's filing for bankruptcy in court, and as if he were being punished by being made fun of. Deeply hurt by the son's joke, he offers his resignation. It's accepted.

A wholesale gut merchant gives him a job and pays him ninety marks more than his old boss, but his business fails shortly thereafter. A while back, Gerhard had taken a buddie fishing with him and the guy had suggested that Gerhard open a refreshment stand at the lake.

Gerhard now inspects his neighborhood from an entirely different point of view. He lives near where the "Silver Gull" once stood. It had burned down during the war and its ruins had been leveled, but a concrete terrace remained along the waterfront, and a small stand with a counter. A wharf juts into the lake there, large enough for ten boats. The property lies on the walkway, which is lined with restaurants on both sides. Gerhard thinks: So anyway! In spite of it! This property is large enough to be noticed by vacationers, fishermen, or people who take their walks here on Sundays.

He doesn't care about the suspicious and hostile looks he gets when he paints the stand and the counter. He tells himself: These restaurant owners to the right and left! They once had to start small as well. And he has as much right to an existence and living space along this walkway as they do.

He opens the stand in March. He sells bottles of beer, Kool-Aid, coffee, tea, cocoa, candy, chewing gum, crackers, sausages, and home-made hamburgers that he cooks on a small gas stove. He is the first one to open in the morning. And when April turns out very warm and the first people pitch their tents on the island campgrounds, everyone very quickly gets used to the fact that it's Gerhard who sells the first refreshments in the whole lake area. Thus they also get used to having their last beer of the evening at his stand, and sometimes they buy a small bottle of liquor in addition, to take home with them. The students from Scharfenberg Island

High School come over to buy bubblegum or — surreptitiously — some cigarettes. Business is going well.

Then the representative of a Rhenish brewing company drops by and says: His company is ready to spend some money in order to be represented at this lake with their brand of beer. Why doesn't Gerhard enlarge his business by adding a garden restaurant? The representative offers a favorable loan for tables, chairs and tablecloths, and he promises to use his influence with liquor and ice cream manufacturers to get Gerhard umbrellas with advertisements on them for free. And Gerhard says: You got a deal! He's going to do it. He immediately applies for a license for a garden restaurant, gets it in May, and by then has his tables and chairs standing under the umbrellas.

At this point, Irene balks: What the hell is this? What's going on? He works from eight in the morning till twelve at night, and throws everything he's got back into his business! He now has more than he had as an employee, but in a way he also has a lot less.

What does it matter, says Gerhard, if now he can be his own boss again?

Irene refuses to wait on the tables. She also refuses to serve at the counter when he offers to wait on the tables: O.K., he himself is going to wait on the tables, hobbling around on his artificial leg, and he'll lie in bed at night with a sore stump.

> DATA: Gerhard marries Irene. They
> live together with Irene's spastic
> mother. Irene becomes a telephone
> operator in the State Department.
> Birth of their first daughter. Heavy
> bombardment of Berlin. Death of the
> mother-in-law and destruction of their
> apartment. Evacuation to Mittwaida,
> Saxony. Birth of their second daughter.

Only Gerhard's mother is of any help. He has her
come from Mittwaida when he's able to rent a room
with kitchen for her across the street. Old Martha
carries the heavy trays to the customers, is very
popular, receives many tips and wants to give the
money to Gerhard because she wants her son to
finally succeed. Gerhard leaves her that spending
money, although she receives a good pension.

At the end of October, a warm month with hundreds
of tourists, his summer license expires. Gerhard
states with satisfaction: He has made good money.
He owes the brewery, to be sure, but he will pay
them off next summer. The one-hundred-eighty
marks for the rent he can cover with his disability
check. All he needs right now is a job.

His landlord suddenly sells the house and the new
owners raise Gerhard's rent by two-hundred marks.
But his vending machine representative promises:
There's no reason for Gerhard to worry. He wants to
become a silent partner in the summer business.
And Gerhard helps him, for hourly wages, to
remodel his old butcher shop, which stands empty
again, into an ice cream parlor. Around Christmas
he learns from his new landlords that the vending

machine representative has changed his mind and signed the lease alone, thus taking over the garden restaurant with Gerhard's debts, and the expected gains. And Gerhard says that he can't even hold it against the rascal for maneuvering him out of all contracts. The guy simply had more money and was able to make quicker decisions. If he himself had been more liquid, he doesn't know whether he'd have treated a short, limping poor bastard like himself any better. He wants to say honestly: He doesn't know.

He finds employment at a local tavern. His boss soon discovers another tavern which he considers a gold mine. He says he would switch immediately if he weren't bound by his contract. He asks whether Gerhard doesn't want to take over his place.

Gerhard doesn't expect a great business, but in Berlin all taverns support their man — if that man doesn't live too extravagantly. You got to play to win, Gerhard tells himself. He wants to try it. He has good relations with the local guys, knows their family histories, can ask how their sons, daughters and dogs are doing, knows what card games they like and knows those who are such bad losers that it's better to let them win.

> DATA: 1946 start of his own butcher shop in Mittwaida. At first Gerhard can't offer anything but herrings, pickles and potato salads. After three years he is surprised by an official investigation of his business. Seventy pounds of meat are missing for which he can't produce the necessary coupons. Usual attrition,

Gerhard argues. But he is suspected of
economic   sabotage.   Since   he   has   to
expect a   twenty-year jail sentence, he
decides to leave East Germany to settle
in West Berlin.

Gerhard   likes   the   evenings   with   Aldo   best.
Although Aldo looks to Gerhard like a Germanic
warrior, he actually has a Spanish mother and her
temperament besides. Aldo is the driver for a liquor
company. He delivers in Gerhard's neighborhood in
the evening, because it's close to his home. Gerhard
invites him for dinner; Aldo has to sing. Aldo has a
baritone voice which keeps all the guests riveted to
their chairs. He sings along with the songs on the
juke box and the audience is excited. Even Irene,
who is usually rarely seen in the tavern, and then
only in a foul mood, comes over when Aldo's voice
can be heard across the street. Recently, she's also
taken to changing her clothes in the evening, fixing
her hair carefully and touching up her eyebrows and
eyelashes. Gerhard notices: she has a crush on
Aldo. He jokes about it to her, and she answers
playfully: Aldo is the man of her dreams; she could
actually run away with him.

Weeks later she holds Aldo's hands, and Aldo sings
to her. Gerhard pleads with Aldo: Don't give her
the eye; don't make an old woman unhappy! But he
figures: they're both the same age, around forty, and
Irene has become noticeably younger looking in
recent weeks. She suddenly takes care of her skin,
wears tighter bras and buys highheeled shoes.

DATA: Gerhard works in a lumber yard
before he finds employment as a butcher

in a chain store. He has his wife and daughters come to him from Mittwaida – in those days a matter of taking the subway from East Berlin to West Berlin.

Gerhard catches them making out in the hallway between the mens room and the ladies room. Irene apologizes: She just got carried away! But a week later Aldo pats her on the bottom in front of all his customers. This is too much for Gerhard: If there has to be hanky-panky, then not in front of him and his customers! He forbids Aldo to come around, but during the following weeks customers come in and report on having seen Aldo and Irene together in this or that tavern, in Aldo's car, or making out on the lakeshore. And one of the customers imitates the moaning which Gerhard knows from Irene when she is about to come. Gerhard tells himself: He has to act; he has to think about something really crazy! He sits brooding behind his bar and serves his customers without enthusiasm. His bad mood is transferred to his customers. Sometimes he starts up from his stool and notices: he's been alone for almost an hour. He has to talk to her, he tells himself every night. He has to confront her, demand an end to this kind of conduct, put his foot down. He formulates statements, but never manages to utter any of them. He lives silently beside her.

And one day Irene leaves the apartment, the kids, and him, to move in with Aldo in Heiligensee. She demands that Gerhard file for divorce, and he obliges. What did he do wrong? he asks in court. Irene says: Nothing. It's somebody else's turn now, that's all.

Brigitte is in her second year of her apprenticeship and can fend for herself; she is about to move out. Monika is pampered by Martha, and by Irene in Heiligensee. Gerhard has to hand over the tavern to a successor. Customers are staying away. There is nothing you can do against fate, he says.

He becomes superintendent of an apartment house in the inner city. Its heating and hot water system depend on an old furnace. During the day Gerhard also works as the handyman in a restaurant. There he does everything from buying meat to dumping the garbage. In the evening, when he meets the tenants on the stairway, they ask him reproachfully: What's the matter with the furnace? The water is cold and they can't take their baths.

He says the furnace is clogged with ash, and there's not enough draft. It clogs up too fast. And he can't spend all day watching that iron monster. You couldn't pay him enough for that.

He asks his mother to come over and loosen the hard residue. But he has to notice: Martha is over seventy, and she doesn't have enough strength for that kind of work. He has to give up the superintendent's job and, after a couple of years, the job at the restaurant as well. He can't run around anymore. He has to walk slowly, take breaks to let the pain in his stump quiet down. He can't stand all day anymore: he needs a job that allows him to sit. He finds one with the Borsig Machine Factory, in the handicapped section. For two years he files small pieces of metal without knowing what their purpose is. He has to process at least five thousand pieces a day, but not more than eight thousand – in order not to depress wages. He dreams about being a gateman, but he learns that there are few of these jobs available in Berlin. There are too many men with artificial limbs in this city. All Gerhard can do is substitute for other gatemen once in a while.

Every six months he visits Irene. Brigitte and Martha take him along. He wouldn't have the nerve to go alone. Aldo has bought a mini-bus and is in business for himself. He seems to be doing well. He's installed a camper on the West bank of the Havel and in the summer he rents out motorboats by the hour. Gerhard can't tell whether Irene is happy or not. She is not unfriendly. She is busy. She never is cordial. Gerhard asks himself: Has she ever been cordial? He doesn't know anymore. She's gained weight. They talk about the children. Both girls have made commitments early: each has a son. Brigitte was also married — to a brick-layer who opened his own contracting business for the construction of weekend homes. Brigitte used to work in his office until she got tired of being slapped in the face every time she couldn't find a file right away. She'd gotten a divorce and plans to start her own secretarial service. She says: She wants to be her own boss. Gerhard is supportive of that, but Irene just makes a contemptuous face. Monika is less aggressive, a more timid kind of person, although she can make people laugh. She always ends up as the center of attention, but she doesn't dare go out in the street by herself. For years she has done nothing except hang out with young bums. Gerhard had finally convinced her: She has to think of her child. If the kid should ever get sick she needs an insurance card. He took her by the hand and brought her to a food service kitchen where she's now working as unskilled help.

Gerhard's mother died. Like every other night, she'd fallen asleep in her easy chair. Usually she'd wake up after half an hour and go crawl under her blanket. This time she hadn't woken up anymore. Gerhard had a used furniture dealer take her things away. He gave her clothes to Irene.

For twenty years now he's been living in West Berlin. He would have preferred to stay in Mittwaida, in Saxony, but he's not the complaining kind. He still expects to have a chance in this city. He's finally found regular work as the third gateman in a highrise parking garage in the suburb of Steglitz. During one of the last busy weekends he made twelve marks in tips alone. That's what he calls good money. The garage is a lifetime job, provided his respiratory system can get used to the exhaust. One of his buddies had to quit because he couldn't talk any more, just screech. Maybe it was just the ventilation system that hadn't been working right. In any case, he'll try his best. He'll drink lots of milk, eat a lot of cottage cheese, and on Sundays he'll take walks in the Grunewald to clean out his lungs and throat—although walking may be hard, on account of his stump.

His boss already knows his name and he greets Gerhard every morning and asks whether there are any problems. When his buddies once took a day off and Gerhard had to run the whole show by himself (fifteen-hundred cars a day!), he didn't raise a stink when the shift manager didn't send anyone to cover for his lunch break. But around four o'clock, when the shift manager had already left, Gerhard musters up all his courage and calls the boss. He tells him: He really has to go to the bathroom, damn it! If the substitute gateman doesn't show up pretty soon . . .

That asshole! his boss replied.

Gerhard is pleased that he can have such a nice and humane conversation with his boss.

He has to move out of his basement apartment. A pipe broke, flooded the whole basement and his apartment never dried out. The dampness crept up the wall next to his bed as high as his pillow and the wallpaper turned black and started to rot away. He's now looking for a room with kitchen and bath on the second floor of a house that sometimes gets a little sun. He hopes that the housing administration will help him find one. And when he finds one he'll go to his union and ask about the possibility of his being sent to a sanitarium with water massages and reclining chairs on a terrace for beauty naps. His last vacation was when they fitted him for his artificial leg—thirty years ago. And when he's had his sanitarium vacation, he'll put an ad in the paper: Sagittarian, fifty-one, with amputated leg, is looking for a lively woman around fifty.

He figures that there must be a lot of good-looking women around fifty in this city, women who've taken good care of themselves and are neither too fat nor too skinny. And maybe he'll find a widow   That would, of course, be the best of luck—a woman who comes with her own pension. But it isn't necessary. He's not after the money.

In the meantime, he drops by Hotte's "Drawing Room" after work to have a beer, a schnapps, another schnapps, and maybe another beer. He throws dice with Hotte, with Klaus and Ursula, or with any acquaintances around who feel like playing a game. Most of the time he has already put a mark in the juke box and pushed C-7, his favorite. He keeps quiet about why he only likes C-7 so much. People don't need to know that. It's none of their business that C-7 stands for a piece of his lost youth. That in it he finds his crazy dreams, his wild desires and plans that have nothing to do with what finally came of them.

> DATA: Early retirement. Marriage to the substitute waitress Clara. Move to a dry, rent-controlled apartment with central heating. First vacation in thirty years: a bus trip to the Black Forest. But he doesn't like it there. The people who run the taverns aren't friendly enough. He returns to Berlin early.

And when he's won a game and had a little too much to drink, and C-7 is playing on the juke box just before he's ready to leave, and after his buddies have stopped paying attention to him, Gerhard can't help but sing along, keeping the beat with his heel against the bar stool: "Wherever on the oceans the tall ships sail away, the German flag is greeted with respect. We want to serve this flag, we want to give our lives for it. The flag is our glorious life, the flag in black, white and red."

CLEVER

No: he doesn't mind questions about his past. Really! He enjoys reminiscing and, after all, he's lived through a great deal. His life holds a treasure of experiences, some that could show the younger generation a thing or two. They've had it too good; unfortunately, much too good.

He hardly remembers his father, a Prussian railroad clerk, except for one special incident. At the time he had just learned to read, he was lying in bed, thumbing through a book on Bismark. His father came over to him and said: That's the right kind of book to read, but if you really want to learn something, read Frida's encyclopedia!

So he takes it out of his sister's schoolbag, looks it over, doesn't understand a thing, but a few technical terms stick in his mind. Natrium Chloride, for instance. During dinner he asks his father how to pronounce it correctly, hinting that he's studying the encyclopedia. His father's mood turns solemn and he tells him that when he knows the encyclopedia by heart, he'll be halfway to being a University Professor.

His mother is a Catholic, excommunicated for marrying a Protestant. She couldn't live it down and in 1918, she hung herself in the basement. Looking back, he only feels the irresponsibility of her act, but then a tendency toward suicide runs in the family. His grandmother swallowed some sort of acid and his sister Frida also hung herself when she was thirty. She was still a virgin and had fallen hopelessly in love with an ophthalmologist who had both a wife and a girlfriend.

In 1919 his father was in charge of organizing troop transport from Belgium back to Germany. One night he slipped off the frozen running board of a railroad car, fell down an embankment, lay on his broken ribs in the cold all night, caught pneumonia and died shortly after. Frida, as an orphaned daughter of a civil servant, gets preference and is hired by the Post Office. She dissolves the household and moves into a rented room. He himself, just ten years old, is sent to a boarding school by his legal guardian, an attorney. Once he's there, he immediately starts thinking about running away. Where to? America, of course! But you need money to do a difficult thing like that. You have to be clever. (Even as a kid, he already knew the meaning of "clever.")

The school is visited occasionally by American Quakers and his job is handing out the information brochures. The brochures are free, of course, but when someone occasionally asks how much they cost, he just says: That's up to you. This gets him ten or twenty cents every once in a while. He's also made a special wire for fishing in the poor box — this nets him occasional dollars — sometimes even a fiver. Even as a kid his sense of justice is keen. The Brothers who run the school tell him that the money is for starving Africans. He thinks they're crazy — they haven't got much to eat themselves so it doesn't make sense to him to just give it away.

He, Atte Nicklisch and Taffe Braun start a gang. Both orphans, Atte and Taffe also have little on their minds except escape. Atte's father is actually still alive, but he's an officer in the Merchant Marine, sailing around between Singapore and

Santiago. One afternoon Taffe, who's as dumb as he's tall, lifts a lock box out of the Principal's office desk. It's open and stuffed with about four-hundred dollars in small bills, probably from the poor box donations. They take off without packing a thing. When they get to the railroad station, they try to buy some bananas to eat on the trip, but the vendor can't make change so they go to the nearest bank. He put all the bills in his shirt pocket and when he gets to the teller's window he pulls one out and asks for change. The teller takes one look at his shirt pocket and asks them to sit down and wait a minute while he calls for the exchange rate.

He has a sinking feeling about the whole thing and sure enough, after a while two kindly looking men appear and turn them in — inside of an hour they're locked in the school basement, naked and set for a caning.

From then on, he really hates the place and its hypocrisy. Do they call this "Love thy neighbor?" The pious Brothers have driven faith right out of him. They're even thinking of transferring him to a home for juvenile delinquents when his guardian decides to speak to his Uncle Utzerath. Uncle Utzerath is a very distant relative, but when he hears of the possibilities, he says: Nonsense! Erich will come to live with me.

He's grateful to his uncle, even though he knows that it isn't costing him anything to keep him. Uncle is the director of the Lichtenberg Workhouse, has a complimentary apartment that's bigger than he can furnish and all his food is supplied by the Workhouse kitchen. The cost of the few clothes that a boy of his age needs is more than covered by his father's railroad pension. Still, he has a real home again and the company of his two cousins, just a year older than himself. They both attend the Humanities High School, a few blocks away.

This time, however, he makes a serious mistake. Since he wants to be in the same classes with his cousins, he fakes his old report cards to make it look like he's a year ahead. At first nobody notices. Then he steals the math, chemistry and physics assignment books from the other section teacher so his homework will look very good. He always raises his hand in class, knowing that his teacher probably won't call on him. It's risky, but he gets away with it until the end of the year. When he's discovered, they make him repeat the whole year. The year after this he has to take it over a third time since the false security of having the stolen assignments made him lazy and left him without much understanding of the basics of the courses.

But Uncle Utzerath backs him up because he's a Socialist and believes that all people are good. Uncle never gets discouraged and always says: Erich will be a success! (And that turns out to be true — in the long run.) He has to admit that his Uncle has a deep sense of justice and always tries to see things in perspective. He himself develops a certain obsession with justice when the authorities decide to kick him out of High School: he'd worked up a heavy crush on his English teacher and would unconsciously stare at her legs or breasts, which she really hated. She wielded a wicked ruler; more than five errors on a dictation and you got it across the knuckles.   Some kids would get punished in installments or after school. The whole idea insulted his sense of human dignity and gradually destroyed any incentive for learning that he may have had.

He decides to enter an apprenticeship program. Uncle Utzerath says: That's your decision; it's your life! He chooses to work in a drugstore, as hard as it is for him. Once, in a fit of anger and frustration, he smashed a full bottle of gold powder against a wall. In his second year of the program he only makes fifteen marks a week, but he sticks it out and finishes. Since he wants to go further, he takes courses at the Pharmacy College in Braunschweig and then gets a job in a drugstore in Cologne for two hundred and twenty marks a month. He isn't licensed to dispense prescriptions, just over-the-counter items, but his boss isn't always too strict about it. He wears a white jacket and feels really great when people address him as "Herr Pharmacist!" Then he makes a mistake which isn't really his fault. Just before closing, an old lady comes in. It's Carnival time and everyone wants to leave early — they're cashing out already so he takes care of her. She hands him a prescription: Olio Olivarium, 15 cc's to use as ear drops. He goes up his ladder, takes down a container and fills a small dropper bottle. Unfortunately, he only follows the first of the three basic rules of pharmacists: look, smell, taste. He figures: What the hell can go wrong with olive oil. A couple of days later the old lady comes back — her ear looks like a cauliflower. He tells her to go back to her doctor for a different prescription. The doctor can't believe the inflammation and is suspicious; he wonders why her ear smells like creosote! Now everything starts to hit the fan and his boss begs him not to tell the authorities that he allowed him to fill simple prescriptions; his payoff is a hundred marks over and above three months salary and the promise of another job.

Erich is so good-hearted that he's a sucker for the deal.

He goes along with his boss and lets himself be fired and censured by the Pharmacists professional association. He's not all that unhappy about the change since his new boss in Wuppertal pays him sixty marks a month more. But when his new boss finds out that Erich's old boss is still paying him, he figures that there is definitely something fishy about the whole deal and fires him. After that he can't get another job; nobody will hire him and he can forget about being a Pharmacist. He moves to Berlin and spends the next five years on the dole; eight marks, eighty a week and his room alone costs him twenty! Those were pretty bad times.

One day Mrs. Arlt, his landlady, asks him if he knows how to paint and hang wallpaper. Sure! he says. He never turns down any work. He starts with the kid's room, glueing down the paper at the edge of the ceiling and smoothing it down to the baseboard, where he cuts it off; then he does the same to the next panel of paper. The paper is brown, with a flower motif. He's already done one wall when Mrs. Arlt comes in, makes a face and says: That looks awful! Nothing fits together! All the flowers are cut off in the middle!

Oh! he says. Was I supposed to match the pattern? Well, I can do it, but I'll need more wallpaper, of course . . . And he slowly learns what it means to wallpaper a room. Painting doesn't come that easy to him either. He starts with the back building stairway. Mrs. Arlt wants the lower half green and the upper half bright yellow.

A dividing line is old-fashioned, he says, hoping that that Mrs. Arlt would agree. No such luck! She wants a nice rusty red dividing line between the green and the yellow; at forty pfennig an hour.

Out of sheer laziness, he starts off painting the green section. When he gets on his ladder to do the top of the stairway, yellow streaks run down the green section, which is still wet. He realizes that he doesn't know shit from painting. How he's going to do the dividing line is a mystery to him. He could have asked someone at the hardware store, but when he was there he'd acted as if he knew absolutely everything! So he just blacks up a string with soot, tacks it down in line and snaps it against the wall. That gets him a dividing line, but it's crooked so he fudges a correction with the red paint. It's still crooked, so he corrects it some more, making the line wider and wider as he corrects it more and more. Mrs. Arlt comes in to check on his progress and can't believe what he's doing! He's forced to go down to the hardware store, after all, and ask for advice. But he still tries to cover his ass by saying that he knows how to paint, but he just doesn't know how to draw a dividing line – a weakness in his art! The guy looks at him like he can't believe it and says: Why don't you just buy a line stencil? It only costs a mark, twenty-five. Hearing this, all he can do is slap himself upside his head!

Mrs. Arlt owns six houses in Berlin, and when he's finished painting all of them, he gets a new job. She says that there are bugs in the Papas' apartment in number 87 — fifth floor, rear. She's confused, embarrassed and, at the same time, furious, and she wonders if he can straighten it all out. He, of course, says: Sure I can! Clever, as always, he buys sulpher sticks and kerosene, gets some old pots, glues windows and keyholes shut with old newspaper and thick glue, and tells the Papas': Afterwards, you'll have to do the cleanup yourselves. Fortunately, Arlt shows up just as he's about to light the sticks and asks him whether that will really take care of the problem. He's quick on the uptake and says doubtfully: You can never be sure. Sometimes the bugs find a path through the thickest walls when they sniff the poison and they end up in the neighbors' apartments. It would be better if the whole house were treated!

At that point Mrs. Arlt backs off a little and says that she'd rather wait and trust in God. Let her! he thinks, and he gets a paper bag and a pair of tweezers and starts collecting roaches behind the pictures and electrical outlets, rejoicing over every little bugger he finds. Then he cuts a little hole in the bottom of the bag, jimmies the opening into the keyhole of the neighboring apartment, and blows hard into the top of the bag. The bag empties, and, sure enough, two weeks later the Arlt woman shows up again, confessing humbly that he was right: Could he go over to 87 and take care of the other apartment? He's glad to oblige, of course, taking care to bring along paper bag and tweezers to find new homes for his little critters. The roaches make him a good living for six months, but then the guys at City Hall want to see his exterminator's license. So in the end he has to apply for Welfare again, and food stamps as well.

But again he uses his imagination organizing the situation.

There are these long hallways in the Social Services building, with doors marked "From Aa to Am," "From An to Bo," "From Br to Di," and so forth, down to "Zu." He goes into the first room, stands at attention, and says: Excuse me. My name is Erich Adler. I lost my job yesterday and the company still has my papers. Would it be possible for me to get a few food stamps to tide me over for a few days so that I won't have to bother you again until my papers come through?

The bureaucratic stiffs find it tough to bend over and cut any red tape. They'd really prefer it if he showed his face every day, and would like it even better if he looked more starved each time; otherwise they wouldn't know what they were there for. But they do give him a few stamps. And then he goes right in the next door and says: Excuse me, my name is Erich Bock. I lost . . . and so on. He continues with this the next day until he gets through the alphabet. It pays. That night he has a wallet full of food stamps. He posts himself next to the soup kitchens, whispering: Food stamps anyone? Fifteen pfennig a piece . . . That does add up!

The government soup kitchens can't afford to offer bad food. They don't dare have stew more than twice a week since the guys who hang out in front are all Communists, and those guys are tough.

When they don't like something they start turning over tables, rip phone cords out of the walls, and throw office files out the windows. And he joins them. Yes, he admits it: In those days he became a member of the Party. After all, he's part of the downtrodden, he wants to improve his position, and he's at his wits end with his limited resources. The Socialists don't do a thing for him; they just talk and seek compromises, which is nothing for Erich Kaufmann. He's in favor of justice—radical justice.

He gets to know 'Sickle' in front of the soup kitchen. When Sickle walks, he throws his left, crippled leg forward in a half-circle, as if he wanted to mow down all the wheat fields in the world. Sickle is a burglar with class. He only bashes in display windows if there's a heavy rain or thunderstorm; the streets are usually empty and the cops can't find any witnesses. Sickle says: Erich, my man, let's pull a big one together! Sickle's proposition is a compliment. He does lookout duty when Sickle breaks into the Berlin-Charlottenburg Administration Building to steal official rubber stamps and Entitlement Certificates for clothing. He fills out a few certificates for himself, picks up three heavy coats, and sells them at a pawnshop. He does all this just for the fun of it—at heart he's not really a criminal. Most of the time he prefers to attend Party meetings and he becomes a member of the Party Chapter Band. He remembers how he was moved to tears when they played "We Are Marching Side by Side." It's something like singing in the church choir.

1933—The night of the Reichstag Fire, and half the city is up. He runs into a comrade, Orje Kelpin. He yells over to him: Do you know what happened? I'll bet Goering's been playing with matches! Two undercover cops approach them, flash their badges, and say: You've made a derogatory remark about the Minister of the Interior. You have to come to the station. Both of you!

On the way he whispers to Orje: I didn't say anything about Goering. I meant Groning! At the station, the officer in charge asks: Communists? They both deny it indignantly and show their unemployment cards. They let Orje go, and he thinks that he's next, but suddenly the cop finds his certification of admission in the CP among his papers.

He's shipped off to the Oranienburg concentration camp, where he's put to work in the fence squad — digging post holes and setting up barbed wire fences in the frozen ground. The guards get a big kick out of letting the prisoners test the possibilities of crawling out under the lowest wire. If they make it, they're kicked in the face on the other side: if they don't, they're kicked in the butt until they go under the wire like sleds, tearing up their clothes and skin. A really shitty game! He didn't like it one bit, and when he was forced to watch them decapitate a prominent Red, he fainted. He just keeled over, got sick and was finally released because they didn't really have anything on him. At that point he tells himself: Never again! It's hammer or anvil, and he's not going to be the anvil ever again.

At the unemployment office they hand him work clothes, a shovel, and five marks for pocket money: tomorrow he has to report out in Rummelsburg where they're building the Autobahn. But he's not that crazy anymore! He just ditches the shovel, and hocks the work clothes. He swears to himself that he'll never see the inside of the unemployment office again. By next week he'll have some dough.

But how? He still doesn't know. He talks it over with Mrs. von Reibnitz, his new landlady, an impoverished aristocrat who rents her extra rooms to bachelors. She tells him: Go downstairs to Willi Knopp. He used to be a Red, too. He runs a lending library from his basement, but only at night. During the day he works the factory circuit selling cheap watches.

Willi Knopp tells him: Erich, you just don't know how to sell things. But he talks so long that Knopp finally agrees to give him a tryout. The next morning they hit the road. Willi gives him a carton to carry and they take the El out to Siemens. Willi introduces himself at the Work Front office, passes out cigarettes, and asks whether he could acquaint German workers with the products of good old German workmanship. During coffee and lunch breaks they display their watches on the cafeteria tables, and Willi begins his spiel: With these new watches, you'll know what time it is at any time, even in these "new times" that are just beginning! Nineteen marks apiece.

Erich, behind his hand, says to a worker standing close by: These "new times" still have only twenty-four hours in a day; and if you don't believe it, all you have to do is take a look at your new watch! Word gets around and he sells three watches right away, five by closing time. Willi gives him two marks commission for every watch sold, so he takes home ten marks. He feels like a king. No, like an emperor! Like the Pope in person! And Willi Knopp tells him: You're an ace!

Of course he is! If selling is nothing more than talking your head off.

He stays with Willi for eight months until he knows all the tricks of the trade. Once Willi takes him to a house where a small sign says: Hausser Watches – Arwed Mayr. Willi tells him to wait downstairs while he disappears into the house. After a while he's back with a new load of watches. Aha! So that's where he gets the merchandise . . .

He tells himself: Erich, why don't you go there yourself? Why not go independent? As soon as he finds some time he goes to Arwed Mayr. He asks him straight out whether he would sell him watches if he were to become Willi Knopp's competitor. Mayr says what a Jew would say: I sell to everybody. And he discovers that Mayr wholesales the watches for six marks apiece. Willi retails them for nineteen marks. Now he knows what he has to do, so he really gets going. He has tremendous incentive. He calls on the factories where Willi introduced him and says: Boys! Knopp tried to cheat you, but now you can buy the very same watches from me for five marks less.

He can hardly describe what happened next. There was a tremendous run on the watches and he doesn't even have enough capital to resupply fast enough, since the workers pay on the installment plan. But Arwed Mayr – he too wants to make money, after all—gives him credit. Now he's really taking off on a clear path. Finally he decides he needs a store, since making the rounds is exhausting. And then comes Kristallnacht—the night he makes his fortune.

He's gone to bed early that night; talking non-stop and running around tires a man out. He's already fallen asleep when breaking glass and shouts of "Jews Out!" wake him up and put him on full alert. Right away he thinks: Edith Rosen! Edith Rosen is a refined old lady who lives on the second floor in a six room apartment all by herself. Every morning a cleaning lady comes in. Edith's dead husband had been an art dealer. He knows the old lady quite well. Once, when Mrs. Rosen had asked him to help her carry her groceries upstairs, he chatted with her and found out that she had really quite reasonable views on social conditions. From then on she'd always said hello to him in a friendly way—even after word got out that he'd been in a concentration camp.

So he jumps out of bed, pulls on shirt and pants, and runs downstairs. Sure enough, Gottlieb Hamann is standing in front of Edith Rosen's door in his Storm Trooper's uniform, beating his fist against it. Gottlieb Hamann studies law but couldn't really be well off. He lives in a small room in the attic and probably has his debts. He's roaring: No more plutocracy! Erich tells him: Tone down. Why are you making such a racket? Don't you know that Mr. Rosen was a very highly decorated Prussian officer?

Jews didn't get any decorations, except by cheating, says Hamann.

Nonsense, he replies. He yells through the door,
asking Mrs. Rosen to open up and show some
photographs of her late husband.

Mrs. Rosen asks them if they would be so kind as to
come in. She looks around for a photograph, while
Hamann is awed by the splendor of the apartment.
He maintains that the contents are stolen from the
"people," but Mrs. Rosen shows him the pictures of
her husband in uniform, decorated with the Pour-le-
merite. Erich says to Hamann: Well? Does he look
like a Jew? He looks like a German, doesn't he?

Gottlieb Hamann still doubts that Mr. Rosen had
done any front line duty, so Mrs. Rosen says that
she'll read him some passages from his war diaries.
She finds the diary where Captain Rosen describes
his meeting with Hindenburg, and she reads aloud
with her low, still frightened voice. Hamann
becomes more and more awed, even meek. He
drinks the glass of Port that Mrs. Rosen offers him,
and then apologizes to her very formally.

My dear Mr. Kaufmann, Mrs. Rosen says to Erich.
How can I ever thank you? At that moment he has
a bright idea: If Mrs. Rosen lends him ten thousand
marks, then her money — with interest — would be
safer with him than with the German Bank. That is
the way he was able to open his shop in the
Bleibtreustrasse.

And now he really gets going! He sells both watches
and musical instruments such as accordions. It was
an old childhood dream of his to have an accordion,
but he'd never been able to have one. Now,
hundreds of them pass through his hands. He has

the best deals in town, since his sense of fairness requires that he earn no more than enough to cover the cost of maintaining his business. He doesn't want to get rich off people who like music, and he's learned from Willi Knopp that you have to go to the people instead of waiting for them to come to you. So he places ads in the dailies offering free music lessons, instruments provided. He sometimes teaches in the store, sometimes in the tavern. The usual crowd is at least twenty people. His goal is to teach anybody who is not entirely unmusical how to play "Take me away, my blond sailor" in an hour. Even the least gifted person can manage the base line, a little um pa pa, um pa pa. And for those who can't get the melody at all, he paints numbers on the keys with black ink that can be washed off later. The numbers run from one to fifty, and he tells his students: Now, sing along! This sells an extra accordion almost every night. After his performance, he tells them: Goodbye, now. I've taught you one song. The rest you'll be able to do yourself.

His name gets around. His competitors are furious and take him to court, charging unfair competition. At one point they actually close his shop, and he has to sell through the back door. Finally, he's had enough of it.

He's been on good terms with Elsbeth Frenzel, one of his sales clerks. He takes her out to dinner, goes shopping with her, and sometimes also takes her to his room. It's true that she's a fan of Goebbels! She says if Goebbels ever came to her, she couldn't guarantee for anything . . . Elsbeth is friends with Erika Wittig, the local Nazi Party leader's secretary.

Erich tells Elsbeth that he'd love to get an appointment with him, and he gets it earlier than he'd dare to hope for: Monday, at four-twenty! He remembers it as if it had been yesterday. At the time he felt somewhat scared, but he thought: It's best to be honest in this situation.

So he goes in, greets the big cheese with a "Heil Hitler," and says: I've been a Communist. He doesn't want to lie about that, and it's in his papers, anyway. Also, that he was at Oranienburg. The Gauleiter doesn't believe what he's hearing, of course, but while the official is still stunned, he continues: You, as a party leader may think about Erich Kaufmann as you wish, but Germans that play music must be both our concerns! Now, can you, a party leader, show me any businessman in Berlin who is doing more for music among the German people than Erich Kaufmann? Regardless of price control and the whole idea of the corporate state!

He then is able to get into a one on one discussion with the Gauleiter, and he doesn't hold back a thing! Finally, the leader says: What are you talking about . . . "Communism?" He thinks that Erich Kaufmann is someone who wants to do something for the German people, so in this sense they share a community sentiment. The party leader promises to do something on his behalf and he keeps his word, too!

Now he has to admit something. Among the Communists, they had all been afraid of each other. And the Socialists were far too lazy to do anything for each other. The Nazis were quite different.

They really help each other, and also help those who have gained their trust. And he's gained their trust by being honest.

The official hassles stopped immediately. He even opened a second store out in Siemensstadt, and he made money hand over fist. That is, until the war breaks out. Then he was one of the first to be drafted. But a friend of his, a doctor, gives him a syringe of anti-gonorrhea vaccine—ten times the usual strength. The doctor tells him: If things get too bad, shoot the stuff right into your dick. The next day it'll drip, and then you tell them that your bladder TB has broken out again. It takes months to diagnose tuberculosis of the bladder, so they'll just send you back to me for treatment!

So he joins the light field artillery in Potsdam. Before he leaves, he says to Elsbeth: Wait for me. I'll be back soon. At first he doesn't dislike the army all that much. The food is good. On the second day they're still running around in their civvies, and the sergeant says nicely: Well, boys, get in line now! Then he asks them: Who wants to become a communications technician? Who wants gunnery? Who wants cavalry? etc. He tells himself: Erich, be clever. Go into the cavalry and you won't have to march! So he gets attached to the cavalry unit and is immediately assigned stable duty. There they are, rows of big Belgian draft horses' asses, guarded by one soldier, who watches them swing their tails. As soon as one of the horses lifts his tail, the soldier races over with a big shovel to catch the apples—so the straw shouldn't get soiled! He asks the guard: Where are the riders? The guard just laughs and says: These days "riders" take care of the horses, clean the stables, and learn to hitch them up to the cannons. And they have to sleep in the straw above the stables. He now tells himself that this isn't going to be too great! Erich, he thinks, you have to give yourself the shot! But before he goes ahead with it, he takes a very big slug of schnapps.

Nine months later a new letter from the draft board comes in the mail, together with an order to report to the Westend Hospital. A doctor feels his genitals while he stands there with his pants down below his knees. Then they give him a sealed letter which he has to take to the barracks. Of course he carefully steams open the letter and reads: Healthy. It cannot be ruled out that Kaufmann simulates! That scares him to death. In fact, it could mean the death penalty! His doctor is willing to write him an attestation, but he declines, resigned: either he'll get lucky again, or he'll go down the drain. But he quickly marries Elsbeth Frenzel: War marriage. He can only get compensation for his stores if he's a married man. They have to be closed, but that's alright. Who on earth is going to be interested in music now? But he tells Elsbeth: Don't think that you can waste the money! You buy gold with every mark you can find.

They send him to the naval base in Kiel. The Navy is a real class outfit. They put him in the hospital for four months to check him out completely. His wife can come to Kiel, so he rents her a room and at night he jumps the barracks wall. This time the hospital stay isn't too bad; except for the cystoscopy: They put a tube, as thick as a finger, up his penis and move it right into his bladder. You could hear his howls a mile away! After his checkup is over, he's sent to Gotenhafen where they train him on an old freighter. His mail number is 13-3-61.

But he's no deadbeat, and goes about making a name for himself. His commander, Prince Leiningen, needs a messenger; someone reliable who can transport the ship's mail and can act as courier for top-secret documents. When the Prince hears that his MA, (Marine Artillerist, although he himself always says 'Marine-Ass') Erich Kaufmann, used to deal in watches and jewelery, he gives him the priviliged assignment. That's how he finds out—ten days earlier than anyone else—that they're going to be sent out against the Russians. The Prince gives him a letter for Princess Leiningen and tells him to expedite delivery particularly carefully. So he asks himself: How come this letter's so important? He uses his old letter opening techniques again. The Prince writes to his wife that he will be forced to attack the land of his ancestors and he is rather depressed at the prospect.

He mulls this over for a few days and wonders whether he should disappear—maybe to Sweden. But then he tells himself that he has possessions in Berlin, and if this regime wins the war—a thought he isn't too happy with—everything he's worked for will be lost. Should he leave everything to the Nazis?

He remains the Prince's messenger for two years. He also makes Corporal and, even before Leningrad, officer candidate. The Prince feels that Erich Kaufmann has authority, but Erich has forbodings about the whole thing and wants to go to his commander and tell him to leave old Kaufmann in the ranks and in peace. But he forgets all about it since he's due to go on leave. He wants to go to Berlin, but Elsbeth, that tramp, writes him that she's really looking forward to his visit, but that, unfortunately, she's pregnant! The father, — in case it's any consolation — has already been killed at the front.

This, of course, knocks the shit out of him, and he doesn't go to Berlin, but to Reval, to see an Estonian girlfriend. He'd been garrisoned in Reval a short while back and had met her, a wheat-blond, immaculate little thing. He spends ten marvelous days with her, although Elsbeth's story still embitters him.

When he returns to his unit, he immediately senses that something's wrong. The atmosphere in the office is icy, and Kuhlmann, the Prince's adjutant, conspicuously avoids him. The next morning, Kuhlmann lines up the men and barks: Kaufmann! Three steps forward! Kuhlmann reads an order from the Navy Commander-In-Chief's administration to the effect that Kaufmann is to lose his position and is busted to MA again.

How could you deceive me? the Prince asks him later on. You should have told me that you'd been in a concentration camp! How do you think it looks for a commander to want to promote an ex-convict to officer's rank? They may go for this kind of thing in the Army — but in the Navy?

He can only try to look contrite and apologize. But the Prince doesn't desert him; he sends him to a communications training course in Deutsch-Eilau.

From there — now a Corporal again — he's transferred to the Army and stationed in Greece. On his way he makes a stop in Berlin. Elsbeth lost the child during a bombing raid: premature birth. He's glad that now nothing stands between himself and his wife any more. It's pretty shitty when you move all over the world and don't even have a solid place to spend your vacation!

However, from now until the end of the war it's vacation time. He's stationed on the Peloponnesus, quartered in a farmhouse near the sea, with a view of Kythera in the distance. He's in charge of two men and a small motorboat. Their assignment is the installation and maintenance of all the telephone lines among the neighboring islands. They don't have much to do. He assigns his men work details, put-puts around the bays in his little boat and sunbathes under the perennially cloudless sky. While there, he sets himself up well with the local peasants, since he knows he wants to come back. He'll buy land and make this his second home. This is where he'll retire.

He's a child of luck — there's no other way to put it. The British land on the Peloponnesus, and he's transferred to Denmark, making the last train out. True, the train is attacked by Yugoslav Partisans and his unit counts nine dead, forty wounded — but all he gets is a bullet in his boot heel. The Tommies finally take him prisoner in Schleswig-Holstein. When they start releasing prisoners after it's all over, the farmers go first. His papers classify him as a merchant, so he tells them he sells agricultural products and without him, the farmers won't have seeds or distributors. They let him go.

He's already written to his wife to come to Flemsburg. They find an attic apartment which they keep nice and warm burning the railroad ties he steals at night; during the day he works as a tinker. But he keeps on wondering what the hell he's doing in Flemsburg when he should be trying to get to Berlin where he still has his inventory, not to mention the gold he buried in the shop basement. If he only knew whether 'Ivan' dug up his storage room! He has to find out. So one night he crosses over to the Russian Zone, crawling through a Russian commander's garden, figuring that it was the last place they'd expect an illegal migrant! He figures right again: He makes it through to Berlin and his store in the Bleibtreustrasse. The store's bombed out and burned out, but the basement is intact. The Russians stole all the accordions, but left boxes of saxophones, flutes, clarinets and harmonicas. And the wall that his treasure was buried behind shows no damage.

Now he needs a work permit and, most of all, a permit for Elsbeth to move to Berlin. Elsbeth, who's still in Flemsburg, is pregnant and can't crawl through a line of guards. He remembers his old comrades who are now getting ready to take over the government, so he contacts them and is greeted like family. It really feels like a family reunion and they don't even ask whether he wants to join the party again: he never left it, and so he's still a Communist. He thinks: Well, it probably can't hurt! He makes a donation, pays his dues, and he's given permission to drive a car. They even give him some help to restore his shop as much as possible under the circumstances. When the Western Allies move into Berlin a short while afterwards, he's probably the only red businessman in West Berlin.

He now gets going again—nothing can stop him. He's only thirty-eight and he sees the best part of his life ahead. He has a son, strength, courage, and ideas. And—he can surely say it of himself—he's clever! He tells himself: Stay humble, sell cheap. He knows that he has to think of something special to succeed, so he starts hiring people who can tune pianos and repair strings. The countless widows of officers and civil servants, sitting in freezing, half demolished apartments with cardboard covered windows, all want to jingle and fiddle again. He organizes this on a large scale and is also one of the first to build music cabinets.

Old radios are lying around everywhere in the ruins and bomb craters, and often the switches, wiring and tubes are still intact; only the cases are demolished. He discovers a nice-looking box on legs in Julius Hopfner's carpenter shop in his backyard. It looks like a flower tray or a sewing box, but, in fact, is an original radio cabinet. He gives it a good looking over and decides, that with a few gold bands glued to the front, the case could be a hot seller. So he gets kids to hunt up old radios for him, and he gives them a harmonica for each usable piece. He hires old radio technicians to repair them and Julius Hopfner to make the cabinets.

Today, people ask him time and again how he did it! How do you start out unemployed and end up a millionaire? Develop a burned-out store into a four-story music business unrivaled in popularity?

He always has some ready answers: That God had come to him every ten or fifteen years with an idea or some money. Then God would say goodbye for a while, telling him: You've received something from me. What you do with it is now up to you.

For instance, the currency revaluation of 1948 was to be expected. Everybody expected it, but nobody knew exactly how it would be done. Anyone with money bought gold, even himself. But it suddenly dawned on him that, if the purpose of revaluation was to stimulate the economy, they couldn't just declare the old currency invalid and give everyone twenty or thirty marks—they'd have to revalue all the money in circulation. Right away he takes all the gold he has and sells it on the black market. Since revaluation hysteria is at it's peak, he gets top prices. On the day of the exchange he has 780,000 marks in the bank, and after revaluation, he still has 78,000. The gold hoarders are wiped out, since there's no more market. The price of gold plummets to a ridiculously low level, but he still has capital. Now he can import merchandise: American record albums, Swiss radios, Spanish guitars. He's the man of the hour and offers the best deals as well.

When the Berlin blockade begins (and he's the first to throw away his party card, of course), when the streets and shops are dark and nobody dares go out, he remembers his old free music lessons. He sends groups out all over the city with accordions and guitars to show that every cabby and streetcar conductor can learn to play an instrument. He has them teach "In the Mood," which is even simpler that the old "Flea Waltz," and everyone knows how to play the "Flea Waltz." The project is a great success. Headline: "Erich Kaufmann Brings Music Into The Blockade." He learns that a good businessman needs popularity.

His colleagues laugh at him, but he doesn't care. His competitors want to make money, money, money, but they can't count to three. They walk on their thick carpets, speak in low voices, dust their Bechstein's—and live on credit. And they make a big deal about his ruining kids' musical ear by selling them cheap instruments—what a lot of high falutin' crap! All he had when he was a kid was a tin can with a hole in it, but he blew it with gusto.

He buys his records exclusively from the big American companies that deal in volume production with a low unit price. Maybe the records won't survive the century, but then who the hell still listens to 1947 productions? And he imports his radios and phonographs directly from Japan: first class goods, even though they're cheap. Even the newspapers admit it, and it's another one of his brilliant strokes of intuition! Periodically he sends a free unit to journalists and asks them to test the model. Then he invites them to a conference in Berlin to discuss the pro's and con's of each model. He pays for all their travel and lodging expenses and they love to come. He's learned that those guys are incredibly grateful if you just sit around the bar with them, buy their drinks, and listen to their life stories.

His big break-through first comes with Rock 'n Roll, and then the Beatles. He doesn't think the stuff is all that bad. Of course, he prefers Verdi operas, or a nice Puccini aria—much more relaxing—but he's a businessman, and he has to disregard his personal tastes. When he realizes that Rock 'n Roll is really hitting the charts, he doesn't try to stem the tide, he rides the wave. He arranges huge parties at his house, with young Rock fans, DJ's and clients as his guests. He invites the best touring bands to come and jam for a little album PR. The noise is wild but the guests go crazy and after the show he asks the lead singer or bandleader to sign a Kaufmann Guitar, which he then gives away to one of the guests. Suddenly, everyone wants a signed guitar, so he fills up whole order books and makes a deal with the bands to authorize signature models.

He also comes up with "The Guitar With The Golden Strings." He includes it in his next catalog and it sells from Berlin to the remotest Bavarian village. Arwed Mayr originally came up with the idea. Mayr had come back from Israel and settled in Frankfurt, dealing in precious stones and metals. Erich orders five hundred gold strings and a thousand simulated gold from Mayr, but Mayr outsmarts him. He delivers four hundred gold and eleven hundred simulated, not making the split clear on the invoice.

Customers discover the difference and Erich has to appear in court on fraud charges; the newspapers are full of the story. He's not totally confident that he'll win the case, so he withdraws one hundred and forty thousand marks from his account and locks them up in the secret compartment of his desk before his court appearance. He's booked and held for five days pending investigation. When he's released on bail, he goes back to his office and finds his secret compartment empty. He discovers that someone named Else Lehmann had a second key made for the registered Schlage lock. Else? Elsbeth? The light dawns! He checks the signature on the receipt and discovers she hadn't even been smart enough to fake her handwriting. The cops search her apartment and find seventy-thousand marks. She insists that that was all there was in the compartment. All charges are dropped. He can't do much about the money, but at least it speeds up their divorce proceedings. He reluctantly leaves the boy with her; there's no room for a child in his wandering life.

At least he's free again. Why should you be married when you're surrounded by so many good-looking women in your own business — friendly, willing women, because they're, of course, so well-paid. Very well paid, indeed!

By now he's fifty-eight and has calmed down a bit. He has more money than he could possibly spend before he's dead. Although he still spends all his time on the business, he thinks he may soon sell out, buy an ocean-going yacht and sail around the world. He already travels quite a bit, taking a five week vacation twice a year. He needs the rest and he's determined to stay in shape. His girlfriend is a twenty-six year old beautiful blond who swims, plays tennis and is a good driver. Once a week he sends her to the Berlitz School so that she'll get the education she'll need when he isn't around anymore. He's taking her to Trinidad this winter. At first he didn't even know where it was. His first thought was Hawaii — Hula-Hula and all that stuff. But he enjoys showing her the world. Last winter they went to Madagascar. That was nice, too. They lolled around on the beach under the palms, and she swam and went water-skiing. Once they even took a bus tour into the jungle. They had a lot of fun with an Austrian in the tour group, even though the guy really went too far once when he pulled the breast band off a native woman to see what she looked like underneath. But the people of Madagascar are very friendly, after all . . .

His favorite place, however, is still the Greek Island of Kythera, off the Peloponnese coast. He stays at his house there every year in late summer. A splendid house, modest on the outside, but furnished with everything civilization has to offer: carpets, its own generator and electric water pump, a small car in the garage, and a small yacht in the boat-house, equipped with the latest in communications gear. He feels at home here, but his girlfriend complains that she doesn't see much of him when they're there because he's always busy tinkering around the house, digging in the garden or talking to the villagers. But that's the way he enjoys himself most of all. If she wants to lay on the beach till she blisters – that's her problem! He likes the Greek people, and he hates the German press for ruining the Greek tourist industry. Just because a few Generals in Athens are trying to create order by getting rid of the same type of intellectual babblers that Germany is also too full of. A friend of his had millions of drachmas invested in a new, excellent hotel. He had to send the whole staff home this year because almost no tourists showed up. That's criminal! The Greeks need an authoritarian government. If three Greeks get together, they don't found three parties, like the Germans, they found five! Politically, the Greeks are children. Economically too. When he had his house built, he had to yell at them all the time and constantly supervise to make sure they didn't screw up the job. And the bureaucracy! The Generals promise to change all that and he supports them.

And, quite frankly, he wouldn't mind one bit if, once again, someone would come along in Germany who had a sense of proportion and humility. Because he himself is still humble. He could have built a house for himself in Germany a long time ago, but he didn't. Why? He lives in a convenient, but not luxurious apartment. Of course he had it decorated with wall-to-wall carpeting, expensive furniture and oriental rugs. There's a bar in one corner, and the wood isn't exactly cheap! All with mirrors and crystal, even though he doesn't drink. All for his guests. But he still has his feet on the ground, which, unfortunately he can't say about the younger generation. His girlfriend, for example, is dying to get a mink coat. He told her that nowadays even the cheapest hooker has a mink coat, and he bought her an oriental rug instead.

Or his son Karlheinz: he's twenty-three now, but not really very reliable. He gives him the combination to the safe, and he doesn't count the money before he goes on a trip, but he wouldn't give him management responsibility. The boy has no head for business. Yes, even though his son is with him now and he himself taught him the business, Karlheinz had been brought up by his mom, and whenever he put his feet down, she would shine his shoes. The boy manages a lot of money, and doesn't understand why his father won't give him a new sports car and a sailboat on the Wannsee. Karlheinz just doesn't know how difficult it is to earn money.

He himself knows it. Because he's learned something in his lifetime and because nothing was ever given to him for free. Nothing!

SO MUCH HAPPINESS

She's so happy, Victoria says, so incredibly happy that she can't believe so much happiness can fit into her! And only yesterday she'd thought that she was in such deep shit that she'd never get out. Yesterday, if some guy told her he was gonna waste her, she'd have given him her bankbook as a bonus.

Yesterday, she gets up around noon, takes a ten-minute shower and eats a ham sandwich in the kitchen. Lucie's clothes are all over the floor, so she picks them up and hangs them on the rack she bought her for Christmas. Her first client is booked for two o'clock, so she has to be at work earlier than Lucie; she puts a double espresso and some chocolates on the night table next to Lucie's bed and kisses her ear, as usual.

Victoria says she hadn't a clue!

The John, a regular in his fifties, is already there, waiting. The madam, that disgusting twat, signals her from the parlor, so she sends him upstairs and goes on in. The old bag's standing next to this guy who's still in his hat and coat—you could smell cop on him a hundred yards upwind. Both of them make a grab for her handbag, but the cop gets there first, dips in, and like a magician, pulls out a big gold pocketwatch.

Victoria swears she's never seen that shitty onion before in her life.

The cop dumps all the stuff out of her handbag onto the carpet, and when she bends over to pick it up, the old bitch kicks her butt so hard she goes flying across the room and hits her head on the piano pedals. That's why she's got this long scrape on her nose that even her make-up can't cover. She screams her head off till all the girls come running out. The madam holds up the watch, points to Victoria and yells: Any of you girls here dumb enough to think some John thought this piece of shit, this worn-out cunt, worth the price of this thousand-mark onion? You think maybe the tooth-fairy put it in her handbag?

Victoria figures right then that she's dead meat around there and has a sinking feeling that Lucie's fat little fingers were stuck in part of this pie. Lucie, that dumpy little lard-ass twit, that chocolate sucking, jealous little bitch!

As soon as she can, she runs right back home and rings the downstairs bell. No answer. She runs upstairs; the door's locked from the inside — no sounds, no steps, no breathing, nothing. Suddenly overcome with pity, she imagines Lucie going down to the corner to buy more chocolates, leaving her key inside and now running from locksmith to locksmith in a panic. Ready to forgive her everything, Victoria runs downstairs and out the door — and the sharp heel of one of her own shoes slams right down into her shoulder. Lucie's hanging out the window, her hair a blonde mess, screaming like crazy: Filthy pig! Shithead! Miserable cocksucking whore! And she's throwing blouses, skirts, sweaters, panties, jeans, slips and shoes. She had to have emptied all the drawers and closets and piled it up, ready to go.

Victoria wishes she were thin enough to sink into the storm drain. To do this to her in front of everyone was the lowest thing Lucie had ever done.

But she pulls herself together, picks her stuff up off the sidewalk, hails a taxi and goes to the train station where she crams everything into three lockers. Now, she figures, she has to keep working — and the quicker the better.

She goes over to the University area and takes a look around. Two of the local girls start hassling her: Just taking a walk? If you're not, move your ugly ass outta here, honey! She isn't taking any crap from those pavement pounders so she pretends she doesn't know what's going on. She jumps into the first car that pulls up, like her husband is picking her up, and turns her first trick. She gets them to drop her off at a different place every time so she avoids the girls who've already divided up their territories on the Street of the East German Uprising. But when it gets dark she decides to go to the movies. She isn't chicken, but she knows that the pimps show up after dark to take their cut and they supervise the territory more closely than the girls. Around eleven she finally heads for the locked door of her watering hole and rings the bell. "The Prince and Princess" is like an evening prayer to her. It's here that she usually has her first cognac after work and Lucie has her creme de menthe.

She's pulled her scarf over her face to hide the scrape, so Peter, the dumb queen, doesn't recognize her at first. Then he says, in his most saccharine voice: And whose sweet paws scratched our valiant Victor?

Shut your stupid face! she answers.

The small room is empty. She doesn't feel like sitting near that motor mouth, so she doesn't take her usual place at the bar and she tells Peter to make it snappy with her drink. All she wants is peace and quiet. The quiet of the grave would be best: a coffin, the cover closed, and that's the end. The tape on the cassette deck is making her nervous too. She wants to think. She has to figure out where she's going to sleep tonight, and where to find a new girlfriend. She needs a pair of boobs to hold onto when she wakes up in the middle of the night and she feels herself getting wet at the thought of Lucie possibly coming in tonight and apologizing.

But Peter is bothering her. He squats at her feet and wants to know how everything happened — the whole thing, every detail. He refuses to listen when she wants to give him a short answer and get rid of him. He brags: He's so happily married! Dan, the divine thing, the love of his life. What he won't do for Danny! Every day he swipes a jar of red caviar so they can have a perfect breakfast. He does their laundry and keeps the apartment so spotless that it looks like a whole herd of cleaning ladies had a field day. Love requires sacrifices — he can't emphasize this enough. And how it's improved his life! He used to be thrilled by just anyone who wanted to shove his hot cigarette up his ass. All he can say is: Everyone be noble, kind and good! It's the only thing that pays. And Danny, that sunnuvabitch, ought to be here already. That tramp's show was over an hour ago. Even the greatest Prima Donna shouldn't need more than an hour to take her makeup off.

Finally Victoria blows her cork: Can't you just shut your goddamn mouth for two minutes? She doesn't care how hurt he looks or that he turns his back on her while polishing the glasses.

Then the bell rings three times and both of them give a start. Peter throws his two-yard scarf over his shoulders and patters over to the door, opens it a crack and then trills: Lucifer, darling! He pulls Lucie into the room. Victoria, staring straight into her brandy glass can feel Peter nodding his head towards her when he says: There sits and pines a loving soul!

My God, nobody's here! cries Lucie, looking around as if she were in the middle of the Sahara desert. She walks past Victoria, wearing a new, expensive dress and, as usual, she has trouble climbing onto a bar stool with her short legs and the tight skirt.

Don't ask me about Danny, Peter says. Victoria was already tacky enough to do it. I don't have the faintest idea where my lecherous darling is leching tonight. Why does he do this to me? To me, the most caring wife and mom he could have! Please, not another word about it anymore. It would only tear up my nerves and my nerves are such delicate little threads. Lucie adds: Not everyone, after all, is as big a pig as a certain . . . With that she turns her gaze and lets it rest on the tips of Victoria's shoes. This is too much for Victoria. She has to get this straight: Have I ever cheated on you? Has there ever been as much as a hint that I'd sleep with another woman? Haven't I done everything you've wanted for the last ten years?

At this, Lucie tries to spit in contempt, but she can't spit. She never has enough spit in her mouth and she doesn't know how to apply enough pressure. Saliva hangs from her lower lip and chin, dripping onto her dress before she can wipe it off with the back of her hand. Peter attentively turns her face towards him and touches it up with a napkin.

That looks funnier than shit, says Victoria. But she doesn't really find it funny. She feels how Lucie must feel behind that face now, a face turning red with embarrassment. A face Victoria's dying to press against her breasts to hide, the way Lucie would love to hide it right now.

As a diversion, Peter says: Lucie, you look really noble in that dress; noble and expensive. I have an eye for things like that. Was there any particular reason you had for buying it?

Heartache, says Lucie.

Oh! God, can I relate to that! Can I sympathize! Every time I'm heartsick I have to buy something new. Once, when a very dear person, a really very dear person left me, I burned all my clothes — what insanity — and bought everything new!

Peter talks and talks, and Victoria thinks: Lucie really looks good. And something bothers her, makes her feel uneasy: The way Lucie said the word "heartache" was something new; she'd never heard her say it quite that way before. A new tone of voice, one that made her perk up her ears like the sound of a strange bell.

Victoria thinks: Maybe I shouldn't be such a pig-headed jerk, pretending it's pride! She's seen Lucie with a guilty conscience, and she knows how bad it usually makes Lucie feel.

Because of that, and only because of that, she says to Lucie: You really look chic.

Is that so? says Lucie, making a face and not even turning around. Victoria says that she never felt more shit upon in her life. What a put-down! What a rejection! She could have bitten her tongue off. She gives herself some advice: Beat it! Pay for your drink and buzz off before the little toad puts another whammy on you. Don't worry where you'll crash. The city is full of people who are glad to share their bed. All you have to do is move around the bars long enough, stay sharp, be patient, choosy and don't take any first offers.

While she's still thinking, the toad asks: May I come over?

Victoria pulls one shoulder up to her ear, but smiles at Lucie and says to Peter: Two cognacs, please.

Two White Russians, says Lucie, also smiling.

Cognac or White Russians, Victoria wants to know what's going on. She wants to know if all she has here is some slimy toad whose croaking has fooled her time and again. One of those who can't live without the carrot and the stick? Because of this, she asks: I want to know exactly whats going down — no more fucking around, no more dodging — Why are you doing this to me?

Because you don't deserve any better!

Because I don't deserve any better? Haven't I
deserved something else, something better? Haven't
I . . .

Yeah, you have, you have, you have, yells Lucie.
And that's what's making me sick! It's always the
same worn-out show!

Victoria says: An honest job—that's something
Lucie never understood, and never will. It was only
for Lucie—and that's the God's honest truth—it was
only for Lucie that she went into that cathouse.
She'd given up her regular job, with its nice
atmosphere and friends because of Lucie's senseless
jealousy. She made the sacrifice even though men
disgust her, and have disgusted her since childhood
when she found out what kind of white, flabby asses
her father and brothers were. She hates men, but
she made the sacrifice in order to stay with Lucie.
No, she isn't complaining and she doesn't need
strokes every day, but she doesn't deserve to be
treated like that by Lucie.

Well, why don't you go away, says Lucie. Why don't
you disappear, hit the road, you cheap whore. Admit
it, you really like getting plugged by some prick for
a quick buck. Take off!

In contrast to Lucie, Victoria can collect a lot of spit
under her tongue, and when she can't hold it back
any longer, can't stand Lucie badmouthing what she
somehow feels is valuable, she spits all she's saved
up right between her eyes. Spit globs hang on
eyeshadow and mascara, running down in streaks,

and Lucie's smugness drips down with it, over her cheeks, nose and chin. Only then, after the surprise finally registers, did she scream, grab one of her pumps and try to beat a spiked heel into Victoria's brain. But Victoria's faster and moves quickly to the side. Lucie jumps up, runs to the bar, grabs a heavy crystal ashtray — but Peter pins down her hand.

The bell rings. Peter gives Lucie a napkin, pulls the ashtray out of her fingers, and throws his long scarf over his shoulder. He walks to the door, saying that he should have quit his job here ages ago. The joint has no class anymore.

And then Yvonne enters the room.

Victoria describes Yvonne: A six-foot tall dame, her blond beehive wig adding another eight inches. A giant lanky body, and a face full of condescension.

Yvonne hands Peter her Nutria cape, looks around the room as if it were a theatre where every last seat was taken and everyone was waiting for Yvonne. She smiles, raises her hand, and says in a drawn, baritone voice: Hi!

Behind her back, the much smaller Danny slides through the crack of the door and stands beside Yvonne like a jockey next to his horse. He's grinning and his eyes remind Victoria of a mutt who's pissed in a potted palm instead of out in the street. Peter quickly shakes Danny's shoulder and asks: Where have you been so long?

Danny backs up a little and the corners of his mouth

turn down. Well, well, well! he says, and pats Peter on the cheek. My little bar-lady wouldn't be jealous, would she? Because—and I hope that you still remember—I don't like that at all! And with that, he slowly pushes Peter's head away from him.

We've been cheating on you, Yvonne says as if she were just looking out the window, watching a garbage truck pass by, but we'd decided to keep it a secret.

Danny laughs. He laughs louder than necessary. Peter asks anxiously: Yvonne's joking, isn't she? Peter's hands are shaking while he pours a Pernod for Yvonne, and whiskey for Danny.

Of course, says Danny, but she has no sense of timing! After all, the whole city knows that she can't tell a joke.

Come on, you guys, says Peter, can't you give it to me straight?

Of course we can, says Yvonne, but you really don't want to hear it. All you want to hear is that nothing happened.

Danny caresses Peter's neck and whispers to him. Yvonne moves a bar stool over to Victoria and breathes heavily.

Victoria always feels a bit crowded by Yvonne; especially by her tits, conspicuously shining out of her decolletage. Tits like that could make Victoria envious, if she didn't prefer to have none at all. "Those plastic tits," Lucie had called them once. That was in Yvonne's bar, where they'd gone to listen to her sing, and where they had to shell out ninety marks for a cheap champagne.

Victoria looks back at Lucie, who's sitting at a table in the darkest corner of the room, turning her back on everybody and chewing her nails. Victoria can imagine her grouchy looking puss.

Yvonne is saying that tonight she did Marlene Dietrich: "Where have all the fairies gone" . . . Does Victoria want a postcard of her—topless, and autographed?

Victoria is angry at her own embarrassment, and at her inability to conduct a conversation without trying to figure out how it will sound to Lucie. She orders a double cognac.

Aren't you putting a bit much in your tank tonight? says Peter.

Tonight I'm on a big cruise and I need a lot of gas, she answers.

Yvonne laughs at that uproariously, and she strokes Victoria's ear, even when Victoria tries to move out of her reach. That's well put, Yvonne says. I have to give you a kiss for that!

She reaches for Victoria's chin with a broad, hard hand, pulls her face towards her, and kisses her with lips that feel enormous and devouring.

Don't do that, says Victoria.

Yvonne imitates her and laughs: I like sawhorses like you a lot. What's your line of work?

She's a hooker! says Lucie, suddenly very close.

Moth! sneers Yvonne. Then she starts chatting with Victoria. She's completely redecorated her apartment and it's really fantastic. Fabulous furniture. Would Victoria like to visit her sometime? She'll brew her a first class capuccino.

Victoria is seized again by this disgusting embarrassment, insecurity and fear, which makes her armpits sweat. She gives Lucie a look to calm her down, make her understand that she has nothing going with Yvonne and doesn't want it either. The chatty type gets on her nerves.

Don't look at me like that, says Lucie. I'm through with you, forever!

Victoria says it was only because of that, because of Lucie's venomous tone of voice and her contempt that she kissed Yvonne on the cheek.

And suddenly Lucie starts to beat up on Yvonne, hitting her with both fists and screaming at the top of her lungs. Then Peter starts to scream, dancing around behind the bar, screaming as if he were coming: Yes, yes, yes!

Yvonne repels the attack effortlessly, keeping Lucie at arms length with a hand in her face. But Lucie just screams louder because she can't reach Yvonne any more, and she swings her fists furiously and aimlessly until Yvonne finally has enough and decks her with a right to the gut.

Victoria instantly kneels down beside Lucie to help her up, but Lucie just kicks at her and keeps on screeching that she's through with her. Then she gets up, runs to the bathroom and locks herself in.

Danny laughs and says: That was a real good jab! Where'd you learn to box? In the Hitler youth movement? Yvonne adjusts her wig and powders her nose. These shitty girls, she says, they're nothing but trouble!

Victoria says that she shouldn't have punched Lucie so hard.

Love? says Yvonne.

Victoria nods a yes, and she feels tears welling up in her eyes. Yes, she says. She believes in love and she takes it very seriously.

How sweet! exclaims Yvonne. What a fossil! She laughs raucously, and Peter looks anxiously at the glasses as if they were about to jump off the shelves.

Danny says that Yvonne doesn't know shit! She has no reason to feel so much above things. All anyone wants from her anyway is to take a look under her skirt, and when the horror of it freezes their pricks, she thinks it's nothing but impotence.

Was the horror really that great? asks Yvonne.

Danny realizes too late that he's given himself away, and he tries to drown out a question from Peter: Love is generous and kind, love isn't fanatic, love isn't frivolous, and love doesn't . . .

Okay, Okay, interrupts Yvonne. You comedian! If I want to listen to true confessions, I'll buy the record.

Why don't you just admit that you keep your 'bar girl' because you're too cheap to pay a cleaning lady, and too lazy to cook for yourself. Other than that, all the cunt does is bore you to death!

Oh, how could I have forgotten poor Lucifer! says Peter, and retreats to the bathroom as well.

In spite of everything, in spite of all the ugly scenes, says Victoria, she takes love seriously. And she also has a private recipe. Biology gave her the idea. She's read it in a magazine, almost learned it by heart because it struck her as so important. There's this Russian, Glysenko, or something like that, who discovered something. He discovered that you can't let nature grow as it will. Mankind invented grafting: two different plants spliced onto each other, and something totally new comes about.

Suddenly Victoria launches into a real lecture. And she doesn't stop even when Lucie and Peter come out of the john, and she isn't fazed by Lucie's sly grin. It's not only important to make sure, she says, that only compatible plants are grafted together, but also to see which one grows better on top and which one below.

Is that related to bed? asks, Yvonne.

It's related to character, says Victoria. And she says right to Lucie's dumb, stupidly grinning face: Yes, I should have beaten you up, instead of comforting you. A slap in the face, a shoe in your shriveled brain and you'd be following me around like a puppy dog.

Yvonne screams with laughter, and she wants to hug Victoria for the lecture. She says she'd love to have such a precious fossil around her more often. Wouldn't Victoria like to just spend the night at her place?

And this time Victoria doesn't anxiously look at Lucie to get her permission, but simply accepts the offer.

Then the bell rings again.

A teenager stumbles in past Peter, pushed forward by a tall, heavy set man around fifty, wearing a dark coat.

Victoria says that she knows the type. She's afraid of their tempers. You have to keep a cool head and stay in control, otherwise they'll rape you to total exhaustion.

Police! Your I.D. cards please! says the guy, while pushing the kid into the middle of the room. He reads the kid's I.D. card aloud: Dieter Harms, minor. Previous offenses: vagrancy, panhandling, soliciting. Does he know what that means? A foster home until he's eighteen. But first, he'd better spill his guts. He'll get three months off his sentence for every confession. Hadn't he been bragging outside that he knew intimately all the clients in this establishment? Well, who does he know here? That one? And the guy points to Danny.

Danny's small, pale face under his blond hair turns even paler, and his voice loses every last bit of strength. Some nerve! he says. He protests against the procedure and wants a lawyer.

You'll get a lawyer, the big guy says. You'll get everything. But until then, you can bitch for all the good it'll do.

I'm not gonna play this game, Danny says, I'm gonna go! But he also readies his I.D. card for inspection. I have a right to be questioned in private, says Danny, and don't believe everything this street chicken has to say! My private life is my own business. I'm a creative artist and my sources of inspiration aren't public matters.

The big guy says that the theatre where Danny works isn't the Royal Shakespeare and he hands back the I.D., saying in a matter-of-fact manner that in any event, Mr. Daniel Schulz-Kelpin does not deny receiving occasional inspirations from this minor.

Peter bawls: Oh, God, Oh God, with this floozy!

Then the big guy takes a closer look at Yvonne, eyeballing her hair, her tits, her tight skirt and right on down her legs. After a pause, he asks: Do you not, gracious lady, have a twin brother? No? That's funny. I remember a boxer—not very talented, but big for a while. This guy had the exact same face you do, gracious lady! Same height and weight, and he had a nice voice—became a singer. But he dropped out of sight in the sleazy bar scene. Oh well, it was a long time ago. But if you, gracious lady, can assure me that there's no connection, or that you aren't him . . . Or didn't you say that?

Victoria says that she finds this whole interrogation upsetting, insulting and unbearable. After the first

shock, which makes her speechless, she swallows a
few times and then explodes: I want to see your
badge, your official I.D.! She says it so hard, so
suddenly and so loud that they're all shocked, even
the big guy.

Listen girl, says the guy, laughing at his own shock,
my I.D.'s the answers I got without any I.D.!

She wants to see his I.D!

Sit down! Fuhrknecht's the name, says the guy, and
he continues pointing at Peter. And who is this
person who seems to think he's naked without his
stole?

It's dear Aunt Peter!

Peter's voice suddenly sounds overjoyed and
childlike. He jumps over the bar and approaches the
guy with swinging hips and outstretched arms. The
big man opens his arms as well. Oh, Humpert!
moans Peter and kisses the guy on the forehead and
cheeks. How long has it been since I've had a
chance to hug you? That was the greatest show
you've ever pulled off! You really sweated this gang
that's been torturing me all night long.

Danny grabs Peter's sleeve and asks: Have you
known all this time who this guy was and never said
a word? You'll pay for this!

Peter is walking on air. Humpert's revenged him,
he says, he's revenged him like he's never been
revenged in his life.

Yvonne says she feels like kicking the guy's teeth in, but alright: An eye for an eye and a tooth for a tooth. They're even now. She's going to go.

But no, no, no! cries Humpert. I most humbly beg your forgiveness! It is, after all, well known what a marvelous performer the adorable Yvonne is. Isn't it understandable that I'd be tempted—just for fun, even though the prank may have gone a bit too far—to compete with her? And the honorable Daniel Schulz-Kelpin really gave me a hard time, almost exposed me.

Who the hell is this guy? asks Yvonne.

A very, very dear acquaintance from very old times, answers Peter.

And Humpert asks all of them for understanding. He's come from an awfully tired party. He got loaded, but without any effect. His wife—yes, he's married, in church and everything. Sometimes he can't believe it himself. His wife, who runs a perfume shop, invited her lady friends over. Disgusting! And he'd been sitting with them, bored out of his mind, until one o'clock, when he thought he'd go out for a beer. On his way, this little runt tries to pick him up (he caresses Dieter, who stands at the bar sipping a coke) and wants to drag him to "The Prince and Princess." He didn't want things to go this far—he hopes that they'll believe him. Besides Peter, other acquaintances may have been at the bar. So, would they please forgive him? And would they perhaps consider reconciling back at his wine cellar where he has yards of champagne? How about a gentleman's party back at his place? And Yvonne, of course, is invited.

Victoria doesn't understand how these guys can come to an agreement so fast, accept the invitation, show enthusiasm and even squeeze hands with this pig. She herself would have loved to continue the fight, but Yvonne is already standing at the door, the Nutria cape slung around her broad shoulders, raising her head again to say goodbye to Victoria: Ciao, sawhorse!

Can't you guys wait for me? wails Peter. I have to keep the joint open till 3 o'clock!

You can take a taxi, says Humpert.

Then Victoria is alone again with Peter and Lucie. Lucie sits relaxed in an easy chair. She has her legs stretched out, and her hands folded in her lap. Imitating Yvonne's deep voice, she says: Ciao, sawhorse! — and laughs.

Oh God, its been a heavy night! says Peter. Did I deserve all that? Don't I do what I can for Danny? For a tramp who drags around with that floozy, and even with that mangled prick, Yvonne? He says that the entire household hangs on him. He studies Danny's roles with him, and knows the parts before that Diva does. He even brings hot meals to the theatre, because the Princess gets a rash on her delicate lips from the slop in the cafeteria. And in bed Danny lies on his back all the time, always demanding the same old thing, while he himself gets nothing. Is that fair? Won't Yvonne be amazed! She doesn't know yet what it means to be on Peter's shit list.

I am doing fine, says Lucie.

Victoria orders another cognac and still doesn't know how things will continue. She doesn't know whether she should show her pride and leave, or whether she's still waiting for Lucie to put her down one more time. Or does she still hope for a reconciliation? — which surely is a rather foolish hope. She takes sips of the cognac. She knows that she has to make a decision, yet she could sit here at the bar all night long. She decides: She'll drink this one cognac, and then she'll go.

Do you have Yvonne's address? Lucie asks behind her. And why don't you have it? Or didn't you notice that that plastic tit was just putting you on?

Victoria doesn't answer. She doesn't know what to say, anyway. All she knows is that she's getting rather tired.

And anyway, didn't you say that you wanted to beat me up? says Lucie. Well, let's have it!

Are you starting again? says Peter, polishing glasses with an indignant face, and turning the music up.

Have a soda on me and shut up! Lucie tells him. She finally wants to tell Victoria what she thinks of this call-girl cow. She wants Victoria to see her own lies. Lucie's needed almost ten years to see through the lies of this lying cow. But now she can see through them, can recognize what is really going on. Its only been a short while ago that the whole thing finally came clear — so clear that it made her ill. This submissiveness, this servile act: Yes, my Lucie, of course, Lucie, whatever Lucie wants will be done, and done the way Lucie wants it. Victoria always gives in, Victoria always understands, Victoria will always go along, Victoria likes what Lucie likes. If Lucie wants to stay another hour in bed at noon — fine! Victoria will put the coffee on the night table. It's all a bunch of horse shit! Victoria's acting the part for a guy that she really wants. Victoria doesn't mean her, Lucie. She only has herself in mind. And how does she know all this? From clients. They've made it clear to her: Victoria enjoys it all! Victoria didn't follow her to the whorehouse to keep Lucie company, as she says, or to spare her feelings of inferiority in comparison to 'Mrs. Civil Servant' with chances for advancement. That's horse shit, too! She came to the cathouse to get a prick into her cunt once in a while! For a few special customers she even does it without a rubber! Secretly, she takes the pill. This is the way she's cheated Lucie for years. And when she talks about fidelity and domesticity, she's really thinking about some guy that she doesn't have, and that she won't get, because you need a good figure for that, not those tit's down to her knees. And you certainly need a bit more culture than Victoria has to offer. No, Victoria is not thinking of Lucie! It's taken her a while to get that into her dumb head. And Lucie says she gladly admits that she doesn't want men. She was pimped by her whoring mother at thirteen and she has absolutely no need for any man. But if Victoria wants to go for a man now — alright, it's fine with her.

Until now, Lucie's been standing behind Victoria's back throughout this tirade. Now she climbs on a bar stool next to her, takes Victoria's hand and kisses it. She says she's thought about it. If Victoria wants to go, that's fine. If she wants to find a guy and marry him, she herself will serve as a witness. But she wants Victoria to know that she loves her — as best as she can, and she wants to stay with her. Because of this, and because she can't stand to listen to Victoria fucking some guy in the next room, she pulled the dirty trick with the gold watch. But she needs a clear decision from Victoria. If Victoria wants to stay with her, exclusively with her, then she'll find her a so-called honest job in the next few days. She doesn't really care what job Victoria has, but well — maybe that's just her hang-up. What the hell! And now she wants to leave, with or without Victoria. But she'd prefer to go with Victoria, if Victoria can make the decision.

Lucie's ordered two more cognacs. As she goes to pay, the telephone rings. Peter picks up the phone, saying: Salvation Army! And then he shrieks: Ernst! No! What? Just married to the arch charmer? Yes, the singer's been here. But if you want to know the truth, she's been fooling around. Yes, with Danny. So now we're in-laws! Right now that singer and Danny are partying at the liquor wholesaler's. Of course he has my permission. Never lose your head, darling. O.K? In a case like this, all you can do is drink peppermint tea!

Then Peter — suddenly breathing very freely — counts the money Lucie gave him, remarking: I'm always so glad when two loving souls get together.

Lucie helps Victoria into her coat, which forces her to stand on tip toes, hails a taxi and even holds the door open for Victoria, something that she's never

done before.   Finally, she puts her arm around
Victoria and kisses her ear.

Victoria says: She's so happy, so unbelievably
happy.   She didn't know that so much happiness
could fit into her.

BEFORE THE THUNDERSTORM

He sat on the terrace and sweated. He'd put his bare feet in a dishpan of water, splashing his toes and rubbing his calf with the cool sole of his other foot. Sometimes he looked at his newspaper, sometimes into the sky. For hours dark blue clouds had been forming in the Southwest, growing thicker now and rising higher. But the brewing thunderstorm hadn't broken loose yet. Every once in a while sheet-lightning flashed — still far away.

He pulled a floor lamp next to his easy chair; although it was only seven o'clock, it was too dark to read without it. He wasn't really reading the paper anyway. He glanced at the personal column in the classifieds a few times and then turned back to the news of the war in Lebanon. The ads had become a hurdle to him; he shied away from them — all because of Koppke, his bookkeeper, that . . . He searched for a word adequate enough to express his rage about Koppke. He couldn't find one.

He knew that Lissi was watching him. She still sat there in the Hollywood swing facing him, strangely quiet and motionless. She had put a plate of sandwiches on the small table next to his wicker chair and was waiting for him to start eating. But he wasn't hungry. He just sweated and nursed his beer bottle, feeling too weak to pour the beer into the glass she had left for him.

Right now he would have liked to be sitting there naked, or standing naked on the lawn of the small garden, cooling himself off with the hose. But he hadn't gone around naked for years — ever since he'd been shocked by the sight of himself in the bedroom mirror: when he pulled in his stomach, shriveled wrinkles showed up beneath his belt line; when he let his belly go, the skin around his belly button looked like orange peel.

He didn't hide from his wife. The fat cells at her underbelly and thighs were further developed than his own — a fact that he registered with great satisfaction. Besides, he had to put up with her varicose veins and the liver spots on her hands: big brown blotches on white skin. He didn't hide from her, but from himself. He didn't want to see his own aging, so he wore shorts and a net shirt. His arms and legs were still all right; they still felt young and strong, even though the rest of him felt tired and exhausted. A swim in the ocean would be the perfect thing for him now.

Until this year they'd spent these same two weeks every July at a small hotel in Altea, Spain. After siesta, he and his wife would drive to the beach to swim for about an hour, her anxious voice always echoing: Don't swim out too far.

He'd swim to the wooden raft anchored about a thousand yards out, climb up on the warm planks, glad to have left her behind. He enjoyed the mobility of sport, and sometimes enjoyed the sight of several well-exercised and naked female bodies. Only those in good condition dared to swim out that far. When he was surrounded by naked women, he'd take off his trunks, trying to inconspicuosly stretch his shriveled penis so that it didn't look like an old carrot that someone had forgotten in a cellar corner. He'd rest for a half hour or more without talking to

the women before he'd swim back to the same
sentence from Lissi: I was so worried!

At the end of every vacation Lissi resolved to buy
binoculars for the next trip so that she wouldn't lose
sight of him. But time and again she'd forget and he
never reminded her of it.

He suddenly had to laugh.

What are you laughing about? Lissi asked.

He remembered that he wasn't on the beach at
Altea, but sweating on his own terrace with
Lissi — under a steadily darkening sky.

Nothing, he said.

Tiny gnats settled on his arms. Irritated, he swatted
at them, their mashed bodies sticking to the skin
and hairs on his forearm. He put his arm in the
water and washed them off. The water had become
tepid from the heat, but he was too listless to change
it. He listened for some sound from his garden; no
bush or leaf moved. There was no wind at all. You
could cut the air with a knife, he thought. Even his
neighbor's poplars, usually in constant motion, did
not even rustle.

At this hour in Spain, he'd be in the mountain
village of Altea la Vieja, sitting in a small bar roofed
over by the leaves and branches of a wide fig tree.
He'd drink his first sherry, feel grateful for the
intimate silence and cool of the place, appreciative of
the friendly distance of the owner, who understood
with equanimity that his regular customer still
hadn't mastered Spanish outside of a few courtesy

phrases. He felt at home there. He loved this hour of solitutde, even if he didn't know whether Lissi granted him the time out of resignation or because she really preferred to lie in the hotel room and read magazines.

For ten years in a row he had driven down on the French autobahn via Strasbourg, Belford, Besancon, and Orange to Barcelona, and then on to Altea, his wife beside him—mostly silent. She didn't have a driver's license, and he was glad; he thought her too nervous and timid to drive. She just listened to music the whole trip and always agreed when he said that those crazy French drivers gave him heartburn. And when they stepped out onto the balcony of their hotel for the first time, looking down at the sea and the wide bay of Altea, she shared the mood with him; he would hug her and she would lean against him as they did in the old days. After that they would forget any tenderness they might have had for each other.

This year he couldn't go. He waited for even the smallest contract, the bank eyeing the cash flow of his construction company with mistrust. He had to let his secretary go and he sat beside the phone gladly accepting any job he was offered: roof repairs, skylight installation, garden walls. Villa construction, his specialty, he couldn't even hope for anymore; out of his whole crew he only had two bricklayers left.

He longed for the wood raft in the bay of Altea and the gray-green roof of the fig tree over the bar in the la Vieja, but he knew that he might not see them again for years. He swatted gnats and thought: I really should change this piss water. But he didn't move and felt the sweat running down his neck into his shirt. The air was motionless.

Please eat something, his wife said.

I can't, he answered, it's still too hot.

Again he looked up at the sky, which grew darker and thicker with clouds. But the rain was still far away.

Something's bothering you, his wife said. She rocked slightly in the Hollywood swing.

I'm all right, he said.

Don't you want to talk to me?

There's nothing to talk about.

Koppke, his bookkeeper, was late coming in this morning. That was something new with Koppke. Koppke couldn't afford to come in late. He'd reached an age where if he was unemployed, he'd be classified as too old for most work. Koppke was usually eager, industrious and exact.

Nine months ago, however, Koppke's wife had suddenly died: heart attack. At that time he'd been good for nothing; he lost all energy, stared into empty space and came to the office—although always on time—reeking of booze. He made mistakes in his calculations, his cost estimates had something insane about them and his clothes were a mess; dirty collars, unpolished shoes. Koppke seemed to have reached his end.

Lissi intervened on his behalf; she almost begged to give Koppke another chance, to keep him at his desk in spite of his appalling state. The man had such a good wife, Lissi said. It's only natural that he's had a breakdown; you mustn't fire him. He's loved his wife, he said only good things about her and they were married for thirty years. When one dies in a marriage like that, the other'll feel like half a person. Such a death doesn't pass without pain. The man deserves our compassion. If we were closer to him, we would have to take him in our arms. Give Koppke a chance!

Lissi's speech impressed him. He'd never heard so many sentences in a row from her before. She'd convinced him to give Koppke a chance, but he had a serious talk with him: Either—or, Koppke! And the admonition seemed to have had an effect. Koppke became clean again, eager and exact. He even started to use cologne.

This morning he dispatched his two workers. One to tear down the foundation of an old boiler in an apartment building—there was the possibility of a follow-up contract remodeling the boiler room into an efficiency—the other to dig up some brick garden paths in a villa that had just changed hands. Two miserable jobs! he thought, but better than pissing up a rope!

Then he waited for Koppke. He knew Koppke had a telephone and could have called in, but he decided to be an understanding boss. He didn't want to yell right away—the way he liked to do to his workers because it disarmed them, pulled their defenses out from under them. He wanted to present himself

quietly: Koppke, what's the matter? Lay it out.
Did things get you down again? I can understand
that. But the thing is — in our present situation . . .

Toward nine-thirty a new, silver-gray Ford Granada
rolled into the company yard. Through the office
window he could observe how Koppke got out
without any hurry, and how he leisurely locked the
car door (as if there were any thieves in the yard!).
Then Koppke pulled himself up to his full height
and stiffly walked towards the office with
thoughtful, measured steps. He opened the door and
closed it slowly behind him, walking up to his boss's
desk without a trace of groveling or humility
expected in one who was going to beg for mercy in
expectation of punishment.

I'm sorry, boss, said Koppke. I had to pick up my
new car.

Your new car? he asked. Until now, Koppke had
bought nothing but used Volkswagens.

Would you like to take a look at it? Koppke asked.
He sounded disagreeably happy, as if his boss had a
surprise coming.

Yes, he said — far too quickly. I'd like to. He got up
from behind his desk, but he had to control himself
not to rush out ahead of Koppke.

He'd almost guessed it when Koppke pulled into the
yard. He'd suppressed a shock and reminded himself
to stay calm, but now he realized that his first
reaction at the sight of the car had been right: it
was the same car that had been on display in the

window of the Ford dealer for the last four months. He'd inspected it several times, touching it, sitting in it; he knew every detail—the light blue tinted glass, retractable sunroof, the rubber-protected bumpers, mag wheels, tachometer, LED gas gauge above the dash, and, finally, the dealers own sticker to the right of the plates.

I'll buy this car! he'd said, four, maybe three months ago. He didn't think that his old Ford would make the four thousand kilometers to Altea and back. He dreamed that he'd pull up in front of his hotel in Altea and in front of the bar in Altea la Vieja in the new car, and the people would smile at him, nod, and snap their fingers in admiration.

He'd already talked with the dealer about a discount in case he'd pay cash. Then he'd negotiated an installment contract. Finally, he had to postpone the transaction because of the deplorable state of his business. But he'd comforted himself by thinking: If I don't go to Spain anyway, the old car will still do.

Now "his" Ford was standing in front of him, owned by one of his employees. It stood for derision, insubordination; he was insulted.

Congratulations! he said and turned back to the one-story office building. Casually, he asked his bookkeeper: Say, Koppke, what's going on? Where did you get the money? He knew that he shouldn't be asking these questions. They were none of his business, but he had the sudden urge to catch Koppke in a criminal act.

I'm getting married again, said Koppke, and began walking beside him — not like a subordinate, but rather like a partner.

You haven't been a widower for a year yet! he said, without being able to stop himself, and he realized immediately that this wasn't his, but Lissi's, sentence.

Yes, that's true, said Koppke, rubbing his hands and looking at them, not seeming to feel guilty. Yes, that's correct. I put an ad in the paper, and then she wrote to me. We've been engaged since last weekend. She gave me the car as an engagement present. Everything went pretty fast.

They sat across from each other at his desk. Koppke took three passport pictures from his billfold. That's her, he said. She owns a five star restaurant in Osnabruck. I'll be her partner, but before that we want to go on a vacation. I'd like to resign, boss. As soon as possible. I know, of course, that I can't simply drop everything here, boss, but if you could . . . As soon as possible. As I said, we want to go on vacation.

Impossible, he said, I need you here. He hadn't needed Koppke for quite some time now.

He looked at the photographs: a well-kept woman of about fifty, with smooth cheeks, a healthy look and witty, alert eyes; a woman with straight posture, but not cool or unapproachable, an amiably attractive smile at the corners of her mouth.

He pushed the photographs back. Suddenly he

hated Koppke. He now realized that Koppke had
undergone a change in the last few weeks, a change
that he'd refused to acknowledge. The sadness
seemed to have disappeared from his eyes and his
smooth cheeks didn't look like dough anymore. He
hated Koppke, and was jealous of this woman who
Koppke had been able to get only because of him, his
boss. During Koppke's sloppy time of mourning he
could have dropped him in disgust like a rotten
potato, squashed and ready for the garbage pile.
Instead, he'd supported Koppke and made it possible
for him to go on living. And this is what he gets in
return!

He was shocked when he realized that he'd kicked
over the dishpan. The water spread out around his
chair and across the terrace.

What are you doing? Lissi jumped up.

It doesn't matter, he said. I wanted to change the
water anyway.

No, Lissi said. Not with your wet feet on the
hardwood floor.

She came over, picked up the dishpan and went into
the house. He looked at her. Her ass didn't interest
him anymore. He thought: She's really gotten ugly
over the past few years. The fat cushions on her
hips had grown larger; fat on her neck and around
her arms as well. When has she ever done
something reasonable? The only thing she ever did
was complain about too much work, while the fact is
that she didn't do a damn thing. A five star
restaurant! Shit!

He went over to the hedge and pissed into the plants.

My fiance owns a house in the South of France, Koppke had said. That's where we want to go. As soon a possible.

He had had the urge to be mean and say: Forget it, Koppke! But then he said: I don't want to be a monster. The company still owes you some vacation. Take it, and take care of everything around here when you get back.

Koppke rose from his chair and bowed: Thank you, boss, thank you. At that moment Koppke became the old employee again, the dependent one.

And now this guy is driving what should be his boss's new car on the same route that he and Lissi travelled for twenty years on their way to Altea. He felt like taking a sickle and slashing into the rose bushes, cutting down his own flowers.

When he came back to his chair a pan of fresh water was standing there. He put his feet into it and the unexpected cold made him moan with pleasure. He bent down and splashed water over his hair and onto his face. He didn't say thank you to Lissi, who seemed to be uneasily waiting for something.

Don't you want to talk to me, after all? she asked again. Something's the matter with you.

No, everything's fine, he said. He knew that if he told her of Koppke's engagement, she would whine: My God! He loved his wife so much! And he would maliciously reply: So what? She's dead. So now he loves another one!

Then I'll go to bed, Lissi said.

He just nodded and turned his head away. He didn't want to look at her again. He was disgusted by her fat. He looked up into the black sky. The sheet-lightning came closer. There was rumbling like very distant cannon fire. He swatted at the gnats with his paper. He thought: The dumbest farmers harvest the biggest potatoes.

He grabbed for his beer. Why don't I ever buy sherry when I'm home? he asked himself. He knew what he'd be feeling if he were sitting, after coming in off the wooden raft in the sea, in front of a sherry in Altea la Vieja under the cool roof of the fig tree: Deep contentment.

He emptied his bottle of beer and waited for the rain. There was still no wind.

UPRISING IN EAST GERMANY

I'm getting out, making my break! There's no way I can stand it here anymore. These miserable clods; I can't deal with them, I can't live with them. What kind of people are they, anyway?

We've waited years for this day; yearned for it. Everyone always talked about what they'd do when it finally came; how brave they'd be, how they'd inspire their neighbors and what they'd say to wake up the clods, cowards and ditherers. And then it came. So what did we make of it? How did we use it? What happened?

I'm ashamed for all of them. I don't want to hear their excuses, their justifications. I should just spit on them — all of them. It's only my instinct for self-preservation that's holding me back. That's why I'll go West — tomorrow or the next day. Forgive me, Marianne, if you find me gone. I'll leave it up to you to follow me or stay here, but please understand my reasons.

You know that I have the flu. I planned to stay in bed this morning, but that Laubschatt woman wakes me up around nine-thirty. (I must say that she's really taken good care of me during the last few days. She cooked for me, changed my sheets and was really the most unselfish and caring landlady imaginable. Maybe she did it because I quit smoking for the last couple of weeks?) She tells me that something's going on downtown — she got it from the baker. I'd heard some stuff on the Berlin broadcast last night but you know how much faith I have in the news; it's like the Jevhovah's

Witnesses — they prophesy the end of the world every night!

However, I get up and put on a clean shirt. Then I almost take it off again, worried that maybe it'll get messed up, but I figure that things probably won't go that far so I just hang my tie back up in the closet. I leave the apartment, but go back again and get my brass knuckles out of the desk drawer. I put them in my coat pocket just in case. You never know!

It's quiet outside, like on a holiday; no cars, no trams.   Couples walk down the street, holding hands.   Then two guys come staggering out of an alley, arms around each other's shoulders, beer bottles in hand, singing "If only our old Kaiser Willy were back!"   I walked down the street towards the Reileck.

The glass police booth in the center of the traffic circle is empty, the door ajar.   A teenage boy wearing weird looking shorts and day-glo socks walks back and forth with a microphone, pulling the cord behind him.   His hair looks like someone attacked him with a curling iron.   He announces that there's going to be a demonstration at five o'clock in the Central Market and we should all be there.   He struts up and down, looking very aware that he's on parade.

The whole circle is surrounded by people, standing or milling around behind the iron railings that separate the sidewalk from the street.   They form little clusters of speculation.   I keep hearing the phrase, "it was bound to happen one of these days," over and over again.   Many just laugh at the boy's weird clothes; I must admit I was amused by the wild colors. Everyone seems interested and curious, but they all just wait. I keep hoping that someone will grab the mike and give a speech. Someone who'll finally let out what we've been holding in all these years, the disappointments and pressures we've all been suffering under. But nothing happens, absolutely nothing. It's like early Mardi-Gras morning, when everybody stands around waiting for the first sign of action they can join, but not knowing where it's going to come from.

Five kids come marching down the street towards the Reileck from the direction of the Marx-Engels-Platz. When they get close to us, they start chanting "Down With the Goatee," (the Chairman suffers for his little vanities!) but it sounds too loud and obnoxious, disturbing the quiet moderation of the debates. Besides, the kids don't look too trustworthy to me, but the crowd smiles at them anyway. The kids, two girls included, grin and look down, repeating their chant. They act as if they don't really mean it. Here and there, people wave at them as they disappear down the street.

Suddenly we hear the roar of heavy motors and three truck loads of Russian soldiers roll by. They're holding their rifles ready, between their knees. The kid with the mike tries to hide in the glass booth; the crowd draws back towards the buildings. The circle suddenly seems vastly empty. For a split-second, my eye catches one of the soldiers; he furiously rams his rifle butt against the floor of the truck. I follow his eyes and see the five foot high billboard of Stalin, now ratty and punctured by rocks.

That rifle butt got to them; I think that they could almost feel it in their necks, because doors are quickly closing and locking all around me. A couple of men who were standing next to me a minute ago suddenly disappear. I can't hear the trucks anymore and wonder if the rest of the army are about to march in on foot, so I put my hand in my pocket, palm the brass knuckles, pull out my hand, squat down and let them quickly drop into a storm drain. Then I start walking downtown. Why should I take any useless risks for those door-slamming cowards?

Pedestrian traffic is slower than usual but there's nothing much to indicate the special nature of the day; only the relaxed air of an unexpected holiday. I run into a guy who's at the University with me and he tells me that there's nothing going on over there. Maybe tomorrow or the next day, he says, with a sheepish grin. He doesn't quite trust me. He doesn't know how things will turn out, how we'll all end up, so he too doesn't want to risk anything. Regardless, I walk to the University.

The big banner on the side-wing is partially torn down. "Marxism is in . . . ," it says " . . . vincible because it is true," lies on the ground. Two workers and three students stand in front of it, arguing. The students want to hang it up again, but they don't dare to do it, while the workers aren't sure whether they should tear down the rest. From a distance, it looks like there's going to be a fight any minute, but they just keep waving their arms and arguing, surrounded by emptiness and open doors.

I go to the Central Market. Hundreds of files lay strewn all over the ground, blowing around in the wind. Two kids wade through them as if they were dry leaves in autumn. I hear that Party Headquarters was stormed—very early in the morning when only a nightwatchman stood guard! A plastic store mannequin dressed up in a prison uniform hangs from a pole in front of the Handel monument. There's a sign around its neck, saying "FREEDOM." Underneath it, the ground is thick with books.

So I keep on walking and finally stop in front of a complex surrounded by a high wall and barred by a tall, solid iron gate. About two-hundred people are milling around in front of the gate, howling and yelling: Free the prisoners! Long live liberty!

I keep my distance from the crowd so I can get a better view of the scene. Somebody standing next to me says that there are only Nazi's and crooks in this prison, anyway, but someone else says that his sister-in-law is in there and that she's always been a good person.

The front liners in the crowd pound their fists against the iron plates. The sound echoes through the courtyard. The prison doesn't seem to be guarded. Bash in the gate! yell a bunch in the back of the crowd and start pushing forward. The people at the gate are squashed and pressed against the iron plates, groaning under the onslaught. Some of them start to curse and yell insults to the rear. Those who can squeeze out the sides and escape the human ram, run to the back and start pushing and yelling: Heave! Ho! The whole group becomes a vortex, never achieving enough momentum to burst open the gate.

A tank rolls up, a Russian officer looking out of its tower. Soldiers are hanging off every inch of it, but its lumbering pace makes it seem as harmless as a farm tractor, so the crowd doesn't break up. They just calm down, suddenly looking like a group of kids waiting for the High School to open up.

The officer grits his teeth when someone in the crowd yells *"Druschba"* and *"Solrastwuitje."*

Now vat you vant? he yells down to the field of heads. A stumpy looking guy climbs up on the tank and starts talking to him in Russian. The soldiers are smoking, and seem just as embarrassed as the crowd surrounding them. As far as I can make out, the interpreter is saying that nothing bad is going on. He's telling the officer that he's a worker and a socialist. He even pulls his party card out of his pocket. It's time to right certain wrongs, he says. Would the Soviets please help them?

Hokay! says the Russian, Vy not?

A platoon of People's Police comes marching up. They carry their rifles on their backs, steel helmets dangling from their belts. Someone shouts towards them: People's Police, don't shoot the people! The iron gate opens from the inside, but the crowd doesn't surge in. As the last of the troopers march through the gate, the first stones begin to fly; one knocks the hat off a trooper. The man breaks out of formation and races for cover in the yard. The gate is quickly closed from inside. The crowd starts laughing, the Russians join in. The officer tries to keep a straight face and makes warning signs to the crowd with his finger, but then he too finally breaks down and grins.

By this time I'm getting hungry, so I walk back towards downtown. I tell myself that it's no use waiting around here, nothing is happening anyway. Downtown is emptier than it was an hour ago. Probably because it's lunchtime. I walk up to a hot-dog stand. The vendor is optimistic: Just wait a few days, he tells his customers, and you'll be able to buy a real Frankfurter from me.

And real Dortmunder beer? someone asks.

A munching woman adds: And soon we'll have oranges and bananas!

A third remarks: No government will be able to hang on to power during this uprising!

I go back to the University in hope of finding someone who will seize the initiative and formulate a resolution to the government expressing student demands.   Or maybe someone who'll propose occupying the radio station, the Post Office or the telephone exchange (things that should have been done already).

Or even someone who'll organize a delegation to go down to the People's Police Barracks and try to talk the men into laying down their arms. But all I find are loitering groups of students, their party pins noticeably missing from their coats.   The conversations are very cautious. My fellow students are obviously afraid that coats will hang with tin again tomorrow and anything they say against the party will be denounced. I turn away.

In a little while, a group of teenagers come running

up, and drag me with them as they race along. Come on! they yell. Come on with us to the Red Ox! They're fighting — liberating the political prisoners!

My knees start to wobble, my legs are aching. The effects of the flu are catching up with me and I can't keep up with the kids. I have to stop and catch my breath. Besides, where can I get a gun? And even if someone put one in my hand, I wouldn't know how to use it.

Around four o'clock I start to follow the others strolling over to the Central Market. A few groups try some chants and slogans but it sounds pretty thin to me. Everyone crowds onto the sidewalk; anyone pushed into the street just waits until he can fit himself back into the stream again.

I take a shortcut through an alley from the old city. Someone is already on the speaker's platform when I get to the market, but all I can hear is static coming from the PA system and the noise of the crowd. A guy standing next to me says that a general strike has been declared and they're waiting for the water system workers to show up. Someone else laughs and says that the whole town is already surrounded by troops.

Suddenly there's yelling and fighting nearby and I see a woman beating on a guy who's trying to break loose. Someone yells: An informer! That bastard sent a lot of people up! Hold him! A couple of guys bar his way and he stops, exhausted. The crowd around him yells: Hang the rotten sunnuvabitch! Yeah, hang him high! He deserves it! Get a rope! A rope!

They drag their prisoner towards a streetlight. Doesn't anyone have a rope? Somebody get a rope! Somebody get a rope! They keep repeating the call. Others stretch from the sidelines to slap his face or spit on him. Why doesn't somebody get a rope?!

A man runs up and tears through the circle around the prisoner. You must be out of your minds! he says. Let the poor bastard go! He'll be tried in a court of law.

Someone yells back: When will that be? And how? Who'll be the Judge?

The prisoner had already vanished behind the wall of bodies when someone says: We could have used a belt, or maybe suspenders!

The voice from the loudspeaker comes through clearer now: No, I didn't walk the Thalmannstrasse, nor did I walk along the Pieckstrasse, or across the Marx-Engels-Platz. No, I walked . . . The voice begins to call the streets by their old names, which I immediately forget. The crowd yells, Bravo! and Hear, Hear!

A new speaker climbs to the platform. After a few sentences, we hear the roar of approaching motors. Armored carriers! Keep your cool, the speaker says. Don't panic! The rolling fortresses come out of the side streets, pushing slowly into the crowd.

We will not fight against an occupation army! the speaker shouts in the direction of the carriers. The soldiers sitting in them make calming, reassuring gestures. Slowly the carriers move through the crowd, cutting a swath that immediately closes up behind them. But on the fringe of the crowd, people are beginning to disappear.

Let's march to the government buildings! the speaker shouts. We want to be part of the community of free and equal peoples! "*Deutschland, Deutschland Uber Alles,*" he starts singing. And the crowd answers: "*Uber Alles in der Welt!*"

I'm being pushed across the market toward the North wing of the church. On the other side I can see a long line of demonstrators march past City Hall. A long line of policemen guard the steps. The crowd and all the people around me are still praising "Germany above all." They ask me why I'm not singing along. I'm surrounded by jubilant people. They raise their arms and recite William Tell's liberty pledge — to each other and to the people watching from the windows above. They're in a Carnival mood.

I want to shout for liberty like all the others, but I'm afraid that their idea of liberty has little to do with my own. So I keep quiet.

The singing and shouting is stopped by a few shots fired at City Hall. Now Germans are shooting at Germans! somebody wails. Pigs! Goddamn Pigs! They ought to be liquidated! Some ricochets whirr by. Everyone around me is falling, screaming and moaning. I duck and run, partly jumping, partly crawling on my hands and knees. State of siege! somebody yells. There are already posters up requiring all citizens to stay home and remain calm!

I take the side streets and alleys, running along with the others, the shots still ringing in my ears. My lungs are just about to give out when two policemen block our way. There are two men and a pregnant woman with me. The woman screeches: I have to get through, I have to get home. My children!

Nobody crosses the main street! one of the policemen says; a lieutenant, nineteen years old, maybe twenty. He's holding a pistol in his shaking hand, his voice shaking too, and his face is white. One of the men next to me says: Come on, buddy, let her pass. He takes a step toward the lieutenant. The pistol smokes, and I hear the shot. The cop whimpers, I didn't mean to do it! The pregnant woman collapses without a sound. The lieutenant turns and runs into a nearby house, the two men on his tail. I run too, stumble, sprain my ankle, but manage to make it up the stairway. The two men are already coming down, a strange look on their faces.

Where is he? I ask.

He's downstairs already! they say.

The lieutenant's on the sidewalk in front of the house, his neck broken. The wounded woman and the two other cops are gone. I run away, limping.

When I get home, my landlady looks worried. Her nephew Paul is here. He's got to get out of the country and she hopes that I won't denounce him. Then she suddenly becomes demanding: Would I mind if Paul slept on the couch in my room? He can't get away tonight and they'll have to see about tomorrow. Of course I don't say no, but I'd have preferred to be alone with my thoughts.

You know him, Marianne. He was introduced to you in the hallway some time ago. He works in the water treatment plant and is treasurer of the local party chapter.

I have to drag every word out of him. The only word he really likes is—Shit! This is his story, if I got it right:

Last night the plant workers elected a committee. Most of the members, as is Paul, are also party members. They go to his place and sit in the kitchen, formulating their demands. They are in favor of a general strike. They send a delegation to management. The negotiations drag on a long time. The delegates don't leave the administration building until the whole plant is surrounded by tanks, and when they leave, they come out handcuffed. That's when Paul decides it's wise to cut out.

There he is, sitting on my couch, sucking on his pipe (which stinks to high heaven), and talking about what is wise. I ask him what he thinks about not taking any risks, about not making a public statement, and about not showing any solidarity with his arrested friends. He just gives me a dumb look.

Now he's asleep. It's four o'clock in the morning. A few hours ago there was still some shooting, but now it's quiet. No one in the streets anymore—the whole city seems asleep. I cannot go to sleep, I just can't.

I know that tomorrow they will all be together again, in the streets, in offices, in factory halls, and in classrooms — and they'll act as if nothing had happened. They'll try to talk about trivial matters, and they'll act like they've all been to a party where everybody got out of line. I couldn't stand that.

~

I've copied the letter to Marianne into my diary. I've talked things over with friends. They don't think it wise to leave yet. H., for example, says that I ought to get my degree before going West. Don't you know how interns are treated in West German hospitals? Besides, I can't get my degree anywhere else as cheap as I can here. H. reminds me of K., who even bought most of his medical equipment here and then opened up a practice in the West. The guy saved himself a lot of trouble!

You know, I think that H. may be right.

These ten stories represent a cross-section of post-war West German society (the title story takes place in East Germany but is a particularly emphatic expression of what may be called a Western attitude). They deal with such protagonists as: a bourgeois divorcee of the "radical chic" who has an hilarious affair with a "real proletarian"; a businessman who weasels his way through life during the Weimar Republic, the Third Reich, and post-war affluence; a self-serving musician who is "seduced" by a young girl; an ex-Legionnaire who tries to compensate for his uneventful life in West Germany by reliving sex and combat in Indo-China; a construction worker who traps his buddy into getting drunk so he can go to bed with his wife; and a lesbian prosititute who is rejected by her jealous girlfriend on the grounds of enjoying her profession. In all the stories, the protagonists try to give an account of their own lives — an account which turns out to be as revealing as it is mendacious. It is Jochen Ziem's particular gift to be able to describe people who are eager to present themselves in a certain way, but who unwittingly expose themselves so completely, that the pretentiousness or downright fabrication of their self-conceptions becomes obvious. *Uprising In East Germany and Other Stories* is a study in the discrepancy between people's self-image and their actual lives.

Jochen Ziem's depiction of West German life is thoroughly political, but not in the usual sense. There is no trace of political or academic language in his work. Ziem uses idiomatic language as a key to understanding the German people. In their own words, characters "explain away, assert, defend, excuse, over-look, whitewash . . . No German author of our day has done better in exploring the peculiar capacity of the German language to turn one's own weaknesses into complaints against others. Each of the tales makes its point by letting a man use his own words to show himself in the best possible light. But the brighter the light, the blacker the shadows . . . Ziem is out to prove that certain aspects of German behavior can be explained out of the structure of the language itself" (*The Times Literary Supplement*, November 21, 1968). By carefully observing his characters' descriptions of their day-to-day lives, one can discern a plausible basis for the rise to power of a man of the intellectual and moral caliber of Hitler in one of the most technologically advanced countries of the Western world. Ziem's work avoids the illusion that there is a private and "purely human" dimension to German life which has nothing to do with xenophobia, storm-troopers, and death camps, and that the sore spots of recent German history were something like an aberration in an otherwise healthy tradition.

During the first twenty years after World War II the West German literary scene was dominated by an attempt to catch up with the Modernism which was suppressed during the years of Nazi rule. The leading writers and critics cultivated a style which was dark, inaccessible to most readers, and almost ostentatiously unpopular. The extremes of "hermetic poetry" set the models and standards for serious writing. It was one of the basic axioms of this literary period that contemporary works of art could not help being dark and complex because modern life had become dark and complex. Realism in literature, for example, was considered not only old-fashioned, but a manifestation of false consciousness.

The literary situation in West Germany has changed profoundly since the sixties; partly under the influence of American Pop Culture and partly as a consequence of socialist qualms about hermeticism in literature, writers have taken to clear and communicative forms of expression. The "New Subjectivism" encouraged authors to resolutely set aside the formalistic sophistication of subtle allusions and excessive self-consciousness in favor of straight-forward statements and unmediated expressions of feeling. The laborious interpretive efforts required for the appreciation of highly esoteric works of art began to be rejected as pretentious and a waste of time. An indication of this change of mood was the noticeable fact that those intellectuals who used to struggle with the intricacies of the twelve-tone compositions of Webern and his followers, gradually relaxed and began to enjoy the music of the Beatles.

Jochen Ziem's work can be seen as part of this broad reaction against hermetic literature. Ziem says, in a recent interview: "I belong to the first [group of] German authors who in the sixties rediscovered the poetry of the trivial (against the poetry of the "absurd," "concrete" poetry, and "pure" poetry), which intended to present the significance of the banal without any political or aesthetic ballast." While the hermeticism of the preceding period was greatly influenced by beliefs such as art for arts sake, or even language for language's sake, Jochen

Ziem produced stories and plays which aimed at exploring the every-day world, and at communicating his findings to others in readily intelligible ways. For Ziem, writing is not a refuge for intellectual aesthetes, but a tool for enlightening himself and his audience about the world beyond literature and art. It is, in other words, a means, not an end.

Ziem shows his characters, through their language, as damaged individuals, as people who are deeply troubled and divided against themselves. His view of West German society could also be called psycho-analytic—provided such a view is imaginable without the jargon usually associated with it. He explains people's behavior in terms of those motivating forces people prefer not to mention: fears of sexual inadequacy, pains and disappointments of social advancement, unresolved guilt feelings, and the emptiness of everyday life, as expressed by the lucid medium of every-day speech. The point of Ziem's stories is recognition: they deal with people who are disturbingly unsettled, and badly torn between something they want to be, and what they actually are. By allowing the characters to expose themselves, Ziem exposes a deeply divided society which has not yet come to terms with itself. And what in the end becomes recognizable is the fact that these divisions run deeper than what politicians or historians suggest; that a people can be divided in other than the obvious ways.

J.K.B and J.A.

WRITERS

Literature,
Philosophy,
Artists' Books,
Art Criticism,
Records & Tapes

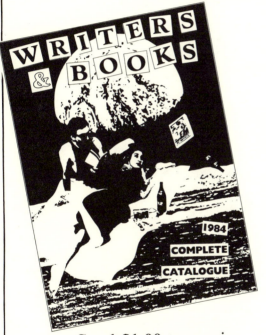

Send $1.00 to receive
our latest catalog
Mail to:
Writers & Books
740 University Ave.
Rochester, N.Y. 14607

 # BOOKS

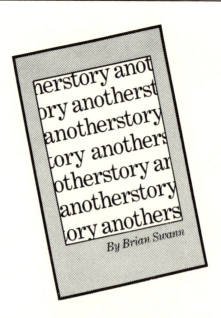

ANOTHER STORY
By Brian Swann

A new novella from a master of the school of experimental fiction. Brimming with realistic details of life in the English countryside and in New York City, a raunchy surrealism invests the protagonist with a kind of purpose as he travels through his time warp, trying to remain sane.

"For Brian Swann, an 'absurdist' writer who actually is one, story comes out of nothing and goes back into nothing. What is left is a residue of voice. Swann's is unique in contemporary fiction: startling, comic, cutting, spare."

Robert Coover

$7.95, 128 pp.   ISBN 0-913623-03-2
26 Signed and Numbered Ltd. Ed. $25.00

ADLER PUBLISHING COMPANY
P.O. BOX 9342
ROCHESTER, NY 14604
(716) 377-5804

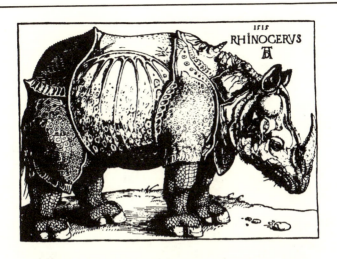

THE PEACEABLE KINGDOM
By Peter Wild

A new collection of poems by one of America's most respected poets and 1973 Pulitzer Prize nominee.

"Peter Wild has mastered the art of writing out of a completely personal world while giving the illusion that he is working with an exterior reality. This wonderful contradiction creates a kind of wholeness of perception that is rare in any poetry. It is a poetry of first the eye, then the ear, and finally the mind." **Diane Wakoski**

"Peter Wild makes you come with him. The journey is exciting, a panorama of change and modulation. The quotidian is shadowed by the unusual; the daily is haunted by the mythic and magical. There is no escaping the grip. Movement, energy, an abundance almost squandered. The clauses pile up; we climb with them. And under the virtuosity, the bravura, the comedy, a kind of sadness; a grasp of the way our lives are led. Peter Wild is one of our best poets. This is a rich book." **Brian Swann.**

$6.95, 64 pp., illus   ISBN 0-913623-01-6
26 Signed, Numbered Ltd. Ed., $15.00

ADLER PUBLISHING COMPANY
P.O. BOX 9342
ROCHESTER, NY 14604
(716) 377-5804

SELF-DETERMINATION
An Anthology of Philosophy and Poetry
Edited by Jorn K. Bramann

A new, interdisciplinary approach to the modern concept of 'self' through the eyes of the great philosophers, writers and poets of Europe and America, from Descartes to Nietzsche, with powerful new translations.

"This collection should be especially useul in stimulating student thought —just right for classroom use. The interesting juxtaposition of different strands of philosophic thought centered on one theme, and a meaningful one at that, strikes me as being a valuable educational tool. And I especially liked the intermingling of excerpts from poets, novelists, and social thinkers as well as philosophers." **Harry Magdoff, co-editor of *Monthly Review*.**

"Treatments of philosophical topics by way of literature are not new; most of them are merely pedestrian, furthering neither the concerns of thought nor feeling. Professor Bramann's study of the Self, however, not only offers new ideas via his deft and refreshingly imaginative juxtaposition of philosophers and poets (try to remember the last time you heard Descartes and Goethe, or Hegel and Byron mentioned in the same breath) but also unearths long and unjustly overlooked material (from Fichte to William Morris to Silesius). *Self-Determination* sets for anthologies of philosophy and literature a new state of the art." **John J. Furlong, Jr.**

$10.95, 256 pp. illustrated   ISBN 0-913623-00-8

ADLER PUBLISHING COMPANY
P.O. BOX 9342
ROCHESTER, NY 14604
(716) 377-5804

OTHER BOOKS FROM ADLER

CAPITAL AS POWER: A Concise Summary of the Marxist Analysis of Capitalism, by Jorn K. Bramann. A beginners guide to Capitalism as seen by Marx and Marxists: a clear and concise depiction of the inner logic of Capital and the development of today's society as the logical conslusion of the initial premises of capitalist production. With political cartoons.

". . . a clear and concise overview of Marxist thought and its relevance today. It does not try to persuade, but just to set out in understandable form the basic ideas of Marx and the Marxists about the workings of Capitalism and the implications for human life. It should be an antidote both to the distortions of the anti-Marxists and to the jargon of the pro-Marxists, and serve as a sensible grounding for further reading." **Patty Lee Parmelee.**

"Capital As Power is nicely compact, has a lot of punch, and should be very useful as a basic statement on the subject. The way classic Marx ideas are blended with contemporary problems and examples enhance both the relevance and usefulness of the book." **John E. Elliott.**

$5.95, 64 pp., illus.   ISBN 0-913623-04-0

UNEMPLOYMENT AND SOCIAL VALUES: A collection of Literay and Philosophical Texts. Issue Number 4 of *Nightsun*, interdisciplinary journal of philosophy and literature. As European prime ministers, presidents and labor leaders wrestle with the concept of a shorter work week and the centenary of the eight-hour work day approaches (May 1, 1886), this timely issue addresses the reduction of labor, environmental destruction and material consumption, as well as self-realization instead of full employment. Poetry by Al MacDougall, Jeff Poniewaz and Antler, short stories by Jochen Ziem and Gerald Haslam, an interview with Michael Harrington Leisure and Unemployment and more.

$6.95, 96 pp., illus.   ISBN 0-913623-02-4

WITTGENSTEIN'S *TRACTATUS* AND THE MODERN ARTS, by Jorn K. Bramann. An innovative study of the structural similarities between the early classic of Analytic Philosophy and the art, literature, poetry, cinema and architecture of the twentieth century.

$15.95   ISBN 0-913623-05-9

43   114